PRINCESS CHARMING

"Oh look!" she whispered; *"it's a baby!"*

(*See page* 63)

PRINCESS CHARMING

"Oh look!" she whispered; "it's a baby!"

(*See page* 63)

PRINCESS CHARMING

by

KATHARINE L. OLDMEADOW

THE CHILDREN'S PRESS
LONDON AND GLASGOW

PRINTED AND MADE IN GREAT BRITAIN

CONTENTS

CHAPTER 1

PANDORA'S IDEA

ONE DULL January morning, when the English Channel looked as grey and cold and leaden as the sullen sky above it, and the Isle of Wight lay like some dark, crouching monster across the bay, four girls sat on the veranda of Idle Pines, with faces as miserable and depressing as the seascape before them.

Penelope, the eldest, a tall girl of seventeen, sat with her knees drawn up to her chin, and propped up languidly against her was the youngest of the girls, Aurora, an elfish-looking child of ten.

Cassandra looked really tragic, for her little pale oval face was sunk between her hands, while Pandora, usually the gay and optimistic member of the family, every now and then sighed lustily.

There were plenty of comfortable chairs on the veranda, but they were all occupied by dogs and cats snoring loudly, and a row of empty plates proved that the grief of the family had not affected the appetites of their pets.

A long polished oak table was set for luncheon in the most sheltered corner of the veranda. An old copper bowl filled with Christmas roses stood in the middle of it, and beautiful old Spode plates and dishes held a very simple repast—a round of cold beef, a carved, wooden bread platter holding a loaf with crust as golden as the butter beside it, and a dessert dish piled with walnuts and russet apples were the only things upon the table.

As Pandora heaved another sigh, Cassandra raised her head and said crossly, "I wish you *wouldn't*, Pan! Things are beastly enough without people making noises down one's ear, as though they were taking gas at the dentist's."

"And if I *don't* groan you say, ' Oh, of course *you* don't care,' just as you did at breakfast when I said it was jolly to have hot potato cakes," said Pan, looking injured.

"Fancy quarrelling about dentists and potato cakes when—when"—Aurora gave a gulp—"when we've got to leave all—this!"

She waved a tragic little hand towards the scene before them—the sweep of garden with its wide, flagged paths, the turfy lawns.

"It wouldn't be so bad leaving if we knew the people who will live here—though I should hate *anyone*, of course," groaned Cassandra.

"Mr. Hay told Wendy that he means to advertise it as suitable for a school or sanatorium," said Penelope. "You know, Father, poor darling, always said he'd make a fortune if he turned the place into a school. It's so gloriously open and sunny."

Everybody relapsed into gloomy silence again, until Pandora leapt up so suddenly that all the dogs woke with a start and began to bark noisily, and the cats fixed reproachful green and amber eyes on the disturber of their slumbers.

"Girls!" cried Pandora. "Listen! Like a flash from heaven *the* Idea of my life has come upon me!"

There was a chorus of groans.

"You needn't be so cattish, all of you—this really is an *Idea*. Oh, do listen, Pen!"

"I don't feel inclined to listen to any more wild-cat schemes."

"But it isn't. It's the most sensible, wonderful, solve-the-question Idea ever known. I can't *think* why none of us ever thought of it before. Why not turn Idle Pines into a school of our own?"

"With you as Principal, I suppose. What a brilliant idea!" said Cassandra.

"It is. Wendy would be the Principal, of course. Father always told her she ought to be the Head of some special sort of school instead of wasting her time on us —and of course ours *would* be a special sort of school. Wendy's so clever and understands girls so well."

"Don't be absurd, Pan," said Pen. "New schools don't spring up all in a minute like mushrooms, and new pupils don't grow on blackberry bushes."

"It's a perfectly *hateful* idea," cried Aurora, looking furiously at Pandora; "fancy, if Idle Pines were really a school—we'd have to go there!"

"Oh, children, don't quarrel about nothing, for good-ness' sake!" expostulated Penelope.

"I do wish Wendy would come back," said Pandora.

"She's coming now," announced Aurora.

Almost as she spoke, Miss Wendell—known as "Wendy" by the girls she had mothered and taught ever since Aurora was a baby—walked on to the veranda.

"Wendy!" cried Pandora; "sit down this instant minute, please, and listen—I've got an Idea that is so gorgeous, it's going to save our lives——"

"No, Pandora, you must be merciful, my child. Here have I been listening to Mr. Hay's ideas for two hours and trying my best to make him listen to mine—which has a *much* larger capital 'I' than yours, I feel sure!

"Mr. Hay has thrown so many wet blankets over me, I feel quite limp. Rory, darling, ring the bell for us."

Aurora stuck a big Chinese gong hanging on the ver-anda, and a lilac-frocked country girl came in with five little covered china bowls full of hot, fragrant soup.

The mist had swallowed up the sea and the island and thrown a cold, grey veil over the tree-tops in the Glen, but nobody seemed to think it in the least odd to eat luncheon out of doors in mid-January.

Phœbe, the little maid, carried away the empty soup cups and brought in a silver dish filled with hot potatoes roasted in their jackets, and as Wendy began to carve the cold beef, four dogs and four cats dropped from their chairs with a thud and took up positions by their respective mistresses, watching with reproachful and pathetic eyes each morsel they ate, and shamelessly ignoring the row of empty plates which showed so plainly that *they* had already dined.

When Phœbe entered again with an apple charlotte and a large silver jug of cream, the four-footed members of the family retired to their chairs and slumbers again, except Cassandra's big black Persian cat, Satan, who liked apple charlotte and cream as much as he liked cold beef.

"We'll have coffee upstairs in the schoolroom, please, Phœbe," said Wendy, "this mist is so depressing."

"Oh, Wendy, do let me tell you my idea!" Pandora looked quite pathetic.

"Come along then upstairs—if you have all finished."

Wendy led the way into the house through a wide hall that was rather like a nice, comfortable farmhouse kitchen. In the cosy inglenook logs were piled ready for lighting, and the oak settles on each side were heaped with cushions covered with chintz of the old, blue check pattern, which went well with the shining brass dogs and the tall polished candlesticks above the inglenook.

A wide, polished staircase led to a long corridor.

Wendy pushed open a door at the end of the corridor into a large room with big windows built out to catch the sunbeams from morning till night, all flung open to the sea.

The walls of the room were pale yellow. The curtains that hung at the windows were of the coppery-gold of the sunset, and the big Chesterfield and the comfortable chairs drawn round the blazing wood fire were heaped with primrose-coloured chintz cushions.

The cheerful yellow note in the room made one think, even when skies were grey and misty, of sunny days, and Cassandra, often inclined to be a gloomy, tragic person, grew more hopeful when she entered it.

A table heaped with paint-boxes, work-baskets, and books, a harp, a piano, and a low bookcase running round two of its walls, showed that the room was a favourite one at Idle Pines.

The dogs stretched themselves before the blazing logs and the cats waited for their mistresses to make comfortable knees.

"If we had a school we could keep the animals!" burst out Aurora, suddenly becoming radiant; for the thought of having to give up these beloved creatures had been far more dreadful to her than leaving Idle Pines.

Wendy gave a jump. "Had a school! My darling child, what made you think of that?"

"It's my Idea," broke in Pandora. "Oh, Wendy, *do* listen! It came upon me like a flash—you know father always said this house *ought* to be a school, and why can't we make it one?"

"Stop! Stop!" Wendy gasped. "Well, of all the strangest things. To think I've been arguing myself hoarse with Mr. Hay this morning about the very same idea!"

"Wendy! Not really!" It was the girls' turn to gasp, and Penelope said, "But how *could* we? We haven't got any money and it must take heaps to start a proper school."

"Well, it wouldn't be a charity school, my dear. Now listen. Because I've been gay and cheerful the last few weeks you must not think I have not noticed your tragic faces, or not understood how broken-hearted you are about leaving Idle Pines. But the place costs far too much to keep up, with things as they are, especially as you must be educated. Mr. Hay is quite sure about that. You know your poor father was not a business man, and he made some unfortunate investments just before he died which turned out very badly—though he believed firmly they would make you all rich if anything happened to him. Now Idle Pines *must* be sold unless we can think of some plan to save it, and the Idea—as Pan calls it—came to me weeks ago, but it seemed too difficult to carry out until this morning."

"Yes, yes. Oh, do go on, Wendy!"

"Do you remember Miss Abbott?"

"That school friend of yours who has the girls' school in Sussex?"

"Yes. To-day I heard from her, and she asked me if I would care to take on her school, which she must give up on account of her health."

"Sussex! Oh, Wendy, you don't mean to do it!"

"Not in Sussex. But a school is very often transferred, and my idea is to transfer Miss Abbott's girls to Idle Pines. After all, Hampshire is only next door to Sussex."

"But, Wendy, it will be hateful turning the house into a girls' school," remonstrated Cassandra.

"More hateful than leaving it altogether, dear?" asked Wendy.

"And who would teach?" inquired Penelope.

"I'm not going to be bullied by a lot of girls. Cass and Pan are bad enough already," cried Aurora indignantly.

"Oh, do stop wet-blanketing, all of you," said Pandora. "Of course, if you'd rather go to a boarding-school yourselves, and find homes for the angels with people who will give them *scraps* and make them lie on the floor —*do!*"

"And if the four girls already in the house are going

to be so quarrelsome, I shall not feel inclined to bother with any more," said Wendy severely. "Now all sit quietly, please—don't interrupt, and I'll tell you what the plan is I have in my head for Idle Pines."

"Can't I speak just once?" asked Cassandra.

"Well, be quick."

"How can we possibly have a school in a house called Idle Pines? It's too stupid for words!"

"Why, it's the nicest part of it," cried Pandora. "Every girl will want to come, thinking they're going to have the time of their lives, and their parents will love it too, for, according to Wendy, parents hate their children to do anything but enjoy themselves at school nowadays."

"We had better change the name to 'Minerva House,' as we're such a classical family," suggested Penelope, and Cassandra looked offended.

"The name doesn't matter at all," said Wendy, "though it will make people curious; and as I mean it to be a holiday school as well, Idle Pines seems to me rather suitable."

"A holiday school!"

"Yes. You all love reading about the camp schools in America, and there are parents who would sometimes be glad to send their girls to a place where they could have a little training as well as a good time in the holidays, and they *could* have a good time by the sea and in the Forest."

"Do you mean we shall have to have girls spoiling everything in the *holidays*, too?" asked Cass tragically.

"If we let them 'spoil everything' it will be our own fault, dear," answered Wendy quietly. "Now, do let me speak.

"First of all, if Idle Pines is to become a school we must all be prepared to do things we don't like and to make some sacrifices."

"I'll give up *anything* so long as we can keep the animals

P.C.   B and I don't have to sleep in a dormitory with a lot of horrid girls," said Aurora heroically.

"Well, my dear child, you certainly can't share one of the best rooms in the house with Pan when it is a school," said Wendy; "it will be difficult enough to arrange things as it is. Besides, I can't have favourites. You will be just one of the schoolgirls when it comes to rules."

"And the dormitory part is one of the nicest things about a school," cried Pan. "Wendy, you *will* let me be in the Fourth Form, won't you? It's the Fourth Form that has all the fun in school stories—the Fifth and Sixth seem so priggy and uppish, and the lower ones are just kids."

Before Rory could make an indignant protest, and Cass and Pen break in with their remarks, Wendy said calmly, "My dear child, there won't be any Fourth Form."

"No Fourth Form! Oh, Wendy, but there *must* be. It couldn't be a school without a Fourth Form, and it will spoil everything!" Pan exclaimed.

"You seem to think we are going to have a school on purpose to let you enjoy yourself like some girl in a silly school story," remarked Cassandra scornfully.

"Do you mean to divide the school up into classes, Wendy?" asked Penelope doubtfully. "Doesn't that sound old-fashioned and remind one of Miss Pinkerton's school and Becky Sharp in *Vanity Fair*?"

"My dear child, I mean to be *much* more old-fashioned than Miss Pinkerton—she was only Georgian, and in some ways I mean to educate my girls as they did in Elizabethan times.

"I can't see any fun in an Elizabethan school," said Pan gloomily. "The boys seemed to get nothing but canings and big doses of Latin grammar, and nobody ever hears anything about girls' schools in those days."

"Girls were educated very much the same as boys were, except for the canings," said Wendy, "and some little girls of six might have easily shamed girls of sixteen nowadays in what they knew of Latin and Greek —not to speak of their exquisite needlework, their accomplished way of playing the viol and the lute, and their singing of madrigals. Why, every one could sing madrigals at sight in Elizabethan days, and it kept whole communities so happy and amused they had no time to be discontented."

"Wendy," cried Pandora suddenly, "do you remember Father telling you about that school he went to see with that method of teaching, 'Montoressi' or something? All the pupils did exactly what they liked about lessons and never wasted time over things they were not inclined to do. I've got a topping idea—let our school be like that!"

"A lot of arithmetic you and Rory would do if you only did it when you felt inclined for it," said Cass scornfully.

"As a matter of fact the school will be carried on according to Montessori methods in some ways," announced Wendy. "Every girl will have to be responsible for herself and show enough grit and ambition to work well without prizes, examinations, or marks. But as for doing exactly as they *like*, I'm wise enough to know that wouldn't answer after teaching certain lazy persons, whom we will not mention, for over nine years!"

"Well, you needn't rub it in so, Wendy," remonstrated Pan, and Aurora said mournfully, "You can't help being born hating to add up things."

"Well, never mind manners and methods just now," began Wendy, once more; "let us go back to what we were saying. Are you all prepared to do your part to save Idle Pines?"

"Of course we are," cried the four girls, "but——"

"No, we can't have 'buts.' I mean, are you prepared to give up your rooms and share all you have with thirty strange girls?"

"Not Father's books," said Cass fiercely.

"Nor the angels," broke in Rory.

"Of course, your father's books will remain as they are in the library," said Wendy gently, "but as for the animals—some of them must be shared, I fear, as I mean to make riding one of the attractions of the school, and any pupil who cannot bring her own pony will, of course, borrow yours occasionally."

Four indignant girls leapt to their feet.

"Let a lot of beastly girls saw away at the mouth of my precious Redskin!" cried Pan, "then that settles it, Wendy."

"Oh, Wendy," wailed Penelope reproachfully, "when you know Snow Queen is getting old, too!"

"I'd just like to see anybody but *me* mount Jackyboy," remarked Aurora unruffled; "they'd jolly well find themselves in the middle of next week, as Mary Ellen says."

"Very well, then—that means you are *not* prepared to make sacrifices and that Idle Pines must go. You all know perfectly well I would not allow any one to pull the ponies' mouths, but it is certainly a good excuse to be selfish," said Wendy severely.

A heated argument followed, in which Penelope wept, Cassandra prophesied gloomily, Pandora stormed, and Aurora vividly described the awful deaths awaiting any new pupil who dared to take liberties with Jackyboy, her own little mouse-coloured Forest pony.

"Of course, Wendy, darling, if you don't *mind* the girls being killed, I'll lend Jackyboy," she said sweetly, and Pan, swallowing violently, murmured, "Redskin is as safe as a cart-horse, and if you are determined to torture us, Wendy, you can let all those girls saw his darling mouth, if you like."

Wendy accepted the offer so gravely that Penelope and Cassandra hastily promised to offer up Snow Queen and Night as unwilling sacrifices, too, and the rest of the afternoon was spent in listening, without interruption, to Wendy's ideas and plans.

When Phœbe brought in tea, it had been quite decided that if Mr. Hay would consent to the plan, Idle Pines was to become an "Open-air-Elizabethan-Montessori-Wendy Girls' School," to use Pan's description. An attractive prospectus was to be drawn up at once for Miss Abbott to send to the parents and friends of her pupils, and the four girls were to be schoolgirls too, and not to grumble about dormitories, Irish stew, suet puddings, nor mind in the least if thirty strange girls walked about Idle Pines as if the place belonged to them.

CHAPTER 2

BUSY DAYS AT IDLE PINES

MR. HAY, the family lawyer, and an old friend of their father, was not at all enthusiastic about the school idea, and if Wendy had not been as good as any lawyer when it came to argument, Idle Pines would have been put up for sale. But after many hours of discussion he gave way, making the gloomy prophecy that Wendy and the girls would be ruined before the year was out, as there were already more schools than girls and the whole scheme was wild and absurd.

"Better sell the place and invest the money in giving the girls an education that will help them to make careers for themselves," he argued, "and there would still be something left to buy a little place for them somewhere."

"But, my dear Mr. Hay," said Wendy, "they can have an excellent education at Idle Pines and keep their old home at the same time, if we manage things properly. It is a risk, I know, but I am ready to risk my own little fortune on the venture; and though I own you are right about there being too many schools already, this is going to be an 'extra-super-school,' to quote Pandora, and instead of spending my old age in the workhouse as you imply, I shall probably be the head of quite a famous school, with fathers and mothers clamouring at the gates for the admittance of their daughters."

"Tut! tut! my dear lady, it is more likely you will do the clamouring. You have had no experience in schools, whatever you know about girls, and to run one successfully you want something besides brains."

"Well, I *have* something—my great-aunt's legacy, and magnificent health, and enough energy to run half a dozen schools. The girls can help too, for though they are lazy sometimes, they are all clever little monkeys."

Mr. Hay was vanquished, and some exciting hours were spent in the schoolroom helping Wendy draw up the school prospectus, which was despatched to Miss Abbott, with the result that twenty-five of the pupils of Hill House School, Sussex, were declared ready to be transferred to Idle Pines, Hampshire, after the Easter holidays.

"Why don't the other girls come?" asked Aurora disgustedly.

"They don't like the part about making their own beds," said Pan—"they're evidently the swanky ones. Wendy, are you going to take *any* sort of pupil, or is it just going to be a school ' for the daughters of gentlemen,' as it says in the advertisements?"

"My dear child, I couldn't endure a snobbish school. Certainly I shall take ' any one,' unless I know her to be undesirable in some way.

The names of the prospective pupils were studied with the greatest interest, and characters were made up for every one of them, and favourites picked out immediately.

"Eve Marriot sounds the nicest," mused Pen. "She's seventeen, and she'll have lots of fair hair, you'll see, and lovely clothes. She'll play or paint really well, too— Eves in books are always nice."

"No, she'll be stuck up!" broke in Pan. "I *feel* she will—Maisie Hill is the one *I* like. She'll really be fun and hate best clothes as much as I do."

"*Maisie!*" scoffed Cassandra; "Maisies are *always* silly creatures! Now, *I* prophesy that Mary Leslie will be the nicest—she won't be silly and she'll be clever without being priggish."

"Then she just won't," cried Rory; "Meg Connell is the nicest—any one can guess that!"

Gladys Shaw was pronounced to belong to a vulgar family, and Isobel Clifton to be a stuck-up person who would want to boss everybody.

No sooner was the school a settled matter than Wendy began to turn Idle Pines upside down. The walls between the largest bedrooms in the front of the house were knocked down, and the rooms became long dormitories, one dedicated by "the classical family" to Æolus, the wind-god, for it was decidedly breezy, and the other to Somnus, the god of sleep. The walls of these rooms were sun-coloured, the floors polished and shining. A wide sea-blue frieze ran round the walls of Æolus, painted by Penelope—who was the artist of the family—with winged youths representing the four winds; and the rugs, curtains, chinaware, and the coverlets on each little bed, were of deep sea-blue, too. Somnus had a soft green frieze, on which was stencilled a design of white poppies, the favourite flower of this drowsy divinity. The rugs were green, and the china, too, patterned with white poppies.

The green curtains and the bed-covers were stencilled with a border of white poppies, the work of the three younger girls, who felt less enthusiastic about the Somnus dormitory before they had finished their task!

A long room in the top story of the house, opening on to a balcony and facing the sea, was christened Sparta, for it was breezier even than Æolus. This dormitory was all white, and had no decorations at all, for Penelope was tired of painting the gods, and the three younger girls, afraid that Wendy would suggest more stencilling, declared that Spartans ought not to be encouraged to have patterns and pictures.

The billiard-room had three more big windows thrown out of it, so that it could almost be called an open-air

schoolroom when the weather was too bad even for
Spartans to sit in the long wooden hut in the garden,
open on all sides, but screened by the sturdy little pine-
wood from too boisterous east winds.

"Somehow I feel sure Gladys Shaw will *hate* being
a Spartan," mused Penelope, and Cassandra added, "So
shall I. Wendy, why can't you call it a sanatorium at
once?"

The only room left untouched was the library, and
this Wendy took for her special sanctum, although it
was to be always open to the four girls.

The domestic staff of the school was soon settled, for
Mary Ellen, who had been nurse at Idle Pines ever since
Penelope was a baby, was elected school-matron.

"You'll have to be called 'Matron,'" said Cassandra.
"Whoever heard of a school with a matron called 'Mary
Ellen'?"

"Excuse me, Miss Cassandra, that I won't and can't
do; there's no luck for them as changes their name
unless it's for a wedded one. It's a thing *They* don't like,
as my Aunt Lizzie found out to her sorrow when she
was soft enough to let the missus call her Kate in that
London place she went to."

Mary Ellen had Celtic blood, and was mountain-bred,
and believed implicitly in the fairies, to which she always
mysteriously alluded as *They*.

Jane, the cook, who was also an old servant, was chosen
as head cook, but she buttoned up her mouth and was
inclined to "put her foot down," when Wendy mentioned cooking was to be included in the school curri-
culum.

"If you ask me, Miss," she said severely, "young ladies
is a lot better at their books than messing in my kitchen
till I'm too moithered even to remember how to boil an
egg! I haven't forgotten the time when Miss Penelope
got the craze for cooking, and the sight it cost in eggs

and burnt saucepans. But I'm sure I'll be glad to oblige
in any way if it's going to help the young ladies to keep
their old 'ome," and Jane sighed virtuously.

Phœbe was to remain as parlour-maid, and two more
country girls, as well as Jane's little kitchen-maid, com-
pleted the indoor domestic staff; for Wendy was determined to keep it small and to make things easy by in-
sisting that the pupils should wait upon themselves.

She then announced her intention of giving notice to
Bates, the gardener, who had kept the whole family in
subjection for years—a tyrant who grew vast quantities
of fruit and vegetables and dealt them out as though each
one was such a rare specimen that it was a crime to eat it.

"You'll never *dare*!" cried all the four girls, aghast at
Wendy's bravery.

"I'll do it this minute," said Wendy.

In half an hour she returned victorious—Bates had
preferred to go rather than let thirty hungry schoolgirls
eat the strawberries and early peas.

"But we *must* have a gardener," said Pen in alarm.

"Of course we must—we'll have Miss Agnes Billock."

"Who on earth is she?"

"She is a lady who answered my advertisement in
The Times. She's willing to take entire charge of the
garden—with a boy to work under her and the help of
all you girls. And she will also be bee-keeper and hen-
wife and instruct any pupil who wishes to learn poultry-
keeping and gardening."

"I don't like her," said Rory disgustedly; "Billock is
a *horrid* name."

"It sounds so ' beefy,' " said Cassandra.

"Well, she isn't ' beefy ' at all, you absurd children—
she is a vegetarian; and I shall write at once and ask
her to come. Joe will stay on and look after the cows
and help her too."

"And who's going to *teach*?" demanded Cassandra.

"I, for one—I'm going to be a working Principal, and Miss Abbott has asked me to have Madame Clément, the French teacher from Hill House, and also Miss Bruce, quite a young girl. Then, if we can get Dorothy Rew and Miss Beatrice Dillon, we shall be all right for our resident staff, and Miss Parriss and Mr. Haddon will come over as usual—only more often—for music and painting."

"Is Dorothy Rew the girl who came over with her father, that old friend of yours, ages ago? She was only a schoolgirl herself," asked Pen.

"She is twenty-two, and her father is dead. She has been training as a teacher of dancing and calisthenics for over four years, and she is wonderful, I believe. She knows all there is to be known about old folk-dances as well as classical dancing, and she is splendid in games of all sorts."

"And who's Miss Dillon?" asked Cassandra.

"She is another *Times* lady who seems to be the very person I want. She would take English and Mathematics, and in her spare time she writes school-books. But whether they are lesson-books or tales about school life I cannot make out."

"How super if it's school-tales!" cried Pan. "Oh, Wendy, you *must* have a Fourth Form; it really isn't fair to her, poor thing, if you don't, and I'd love to be in the book as the jolliest girl or something."

"She won't put *you* in," scoffed Cassandra. "She'll want something more original. I should think that Billock person would be more interesting than we are."

The busy days flew by, and in April, all the preparations were complete. In the first week of May the "Open-air-Elizabethan-Montessori-Wendy School" opened its sunny doors to receive its first pupils.

CHAPTER 3

THE SPARTANS

To Pen's disappointment, Eve Marriot was dumpy, with short dark hair, and her clothes were put on anyhow. She informed everybody almost immediately that she couldn't play a note nor draw a line to save her life, and she had come to Idle Pines because it seemed to be "a decent open-air school where you learnt something besides parlour-tricks." In two years' time she was going to be her brother's housekeeper in Canada, and she wished to learn all she could about poultry-keeping, cooking, etc. "I wanted to go as pupil at a poultry-farm," she said, "but Dad simply wouldn't hear of my leaving school at sixteen—so here I am."

Mary Leslie was a fluffy girl with very big blue eyes, and an inclination to pose.

To Cassandra's disgust, she asked her "where on earth she got her weird name from—and whether she was any relation to the boy that stood on the burning deck?" A flippant remark which shocked the scholarly Cassandra.

Maisie Hill wore spectacles and looked too stolid ever to be able to live up to the character Pandora had made for her, and Meg Connell—an important and very pretty person just arrived at her teens—thought it her duty to snub the advances of Aurora, whom anybody could see was only "a kid of about ten."

The rest of the pupils seemed all alike to the four girls during the first moments which followed their arrival, for they all felt shy and bewildered amongst so many strangers, and it was annoying to see these noisy, laugh-

ing, chattering creatures trooping upstairs, banging
doors and taking possession of the house as though it
belonged to them.

The beloved cats liked the noise and disturbance as
little as their mistresses, and showed so much distress
that they all had to be carried to the sanctuary of the
library, where they were comforted with beds made of
the new cushions and Wendy's old garden coat, while
the dogs were persuaded to occupy the most comfortable
chairs and "be angels," and endure thirty horrid girls
because they meant bread and butter for their mistresses,
not to speak of bones and biscuits and fish for the angels
themselves.

Wendy, coming in later with several rather pompous
fathers, who had brought their daughters to school
themselves and were inclined for a smoke and a chat
before leaving, found this angelic, snoring company in
complete occupation of the head mistress's sanctum, and
a row of empty plates and saucers on the floor made her
feel, as she indignantly told the girls afterwards, "more
like a person in charge of a Home for Cats and Dogs,
than the Principal of Idle Pines."

Miss Agnes Billock had arrived the day before, and
Pandora, who was the first to see her stout ankles de-
scending from the pony-carriage, rushed upstairs and
cried, "Girls, she *is* Billock—she couldn't be anything
else; and Billy for short. Come and see her—do!"

Miss Billock was immense; in fact, nothing was small
about her except the absurd little felt hat she wore
perched on her weather-beaten forehead. She was dressed
in a short tweed skirt and coat and a flannel shirt, and
wore a man's boots, and shouldered her own luggage to
Bates's old cottage as though it were a hand-bag.

She was to sleep in the cottage and have meals with the
school, and her furniture consisted of a bed, a clock, an
armchair, and a huge box of books.

"I'd rather sleep in a tub than a cottage," she explained loudly, "but as the rain-tub is the only one that would fit me, and I can't do without that, I must put up with with the cottage, but for goodness' sake don't crowd me up with furniture."

Madame Clément was elegant and not too young; Miss Abbott had a horror of flighty Mesdemoiselles; but Miss Bruce was young and very earnest and kind, and Miss Beatrice Dillon was a tall person with brilliant dark eyes and a very quiet manner.

Dorothy Rew was as pretty and jolly as when she stayed at Idle Pines a schoolgirl herself years before, and her first command was that nobody should call her Miss Rew, but just Dorothy.

"'Miss' is such a horrid appellation," she said. "I shouldn't mind if I were called 'Mistress Dorothy,' but 'Miss' makes one feel an old maid, a thing I don't mean to be, so you can all call me Dorothy; but if it makes you disrespectful in other ways, I know an exercise to give you as a punishment that will make your muscles ache for weeks!"

Dorothy was pronounced to be "a good sort" by the new girls, Miss Billock "an absurd freak," Miss Bruce "colourless," Madame Clément "chic but a Gorgon," Miss Dillon "the quiet sort that suddenly pounces," and Wendy "a nice old thing."

This last verdict was received by Wendy's four old pupils with indignation, and Cassandra said wrathfully, "Miss Wendell is not a *Thing*—she is a Personage, if you want to know, and as for being *old*, she will never be *that*."

"Oh," said a fair girl named Pauline, who had no idea Cassandra had any connection with Idle Pines nor Wendy, for the conversation took place on the veranda soon after tea on the first day, "so heroine-worship is going to begin at once. Well, *I* shan't visit the shrine. I think

Miss Wendell is quite nice, but rather a dowdy-looking person to be a head mistress."

Indignant protests from Wendy's faithful followers were stopped by a summons to the school-room; for parents and visitors had at last departed, and Miss Wendell wished to say a few words to her new pupils before supper-time.

To be a new girl is always a rather exciting experience; but to be a new girl at a *new* school is more exciting still, and when they all filed into the long school-room, with three windows open to a golden sea of gorse and three to the deep blue of the English Channel, and every window-ledge filled with bowls of pale primroses, they all felt "more holidayish than schoolish" as somebody whispered to somebody else.

Wendy sat in the middle of them all in a friendly big-sisterly sort of way, and each girl acknowledged to herself that the head mistress of Idle Pines School *did* look rather a Personage in some mysterious way.

"I don't want to say very much, children," she said, and the sound of her voice when she used the last word made even the senior girls not resent being called "children" at all.

"You all know this is a *new* school. I cannot tell you tales about brilliant and distinguished pupils who have brought honour to it before; I can only ask you to make it distinguished by your own efforts.

"There are already a great many open-air schools where the pupils learn to be useful as well as clever; but I think this one will perhaps be a little different from them all, because I particularly wish to have a different feeling here between the pupils and those who so kindly give up their valuable time to teaching them. When I went to school in England it was the fashion either to ' quiz '—that is a nice old-fashioned word for ' criticise ' —or to adore the mistresses. When I went to Paris it was the same; and the same, too, when I went to Germany to finish.

"In all schools it seems to be the old tale—Miss So-and-So is either a 'perfect darling' or 'a mean old thing.' Now," she smiled whimsically, "I don't consider myself 'a mean old thing,' and if any of you should consider me a 'perfect darling,' I expect you to show it by keeping the simple rules of the school without worrying me to enforce them too sternly. I think there should be a comradeship between pupil and teacher. And that is the feelings I want to establish here.

"With so much to learn and so much to do, we will not be foolish enough to waste time on impositions. We will have a school without them, and without marks, too, for they cause jealousy; and surely girls with even ordinary brains can work for work's sake. I shall not give the ordinary school prizes either, although there are three distinctions to be won in the school—the *cordon bleu* at the end of each year for the pupil who shows the most ability in housecraft, a very necessary accomplishment in these days. A silver medal for the best all-round student, and a year's scholarship for the pupil most distinguished in classics—to be called the Richard Charles Barron Scholarship."

Wendy glanced lovingly at her four old pupils when she announced the classical scholarship, and they all longed to jump up and hug her; for it was so like her to let the memory of their beloved father bring honour to the home he had loved so much.

"Perhaps," continued Wendy, "a school without 'mean old things' to criticise, 'perfect darlings' to adore, and neither marks nor prizes to stimulate one's energies seems to you a dull sort of place; but if you *are* dull, my children, it will certainly be your own fault, for I mean to make Idle Pines as busy and happy as a bee-hive.

"I think all of you have been to school before except

four girls"—she looked at her old pupils sitting rather
forlornly amongst the invaders of their home—"and
most of you have the usual schoolgirl grievances. To-
morrow I shall elect two prefects, and in a week's time
I wish these prefects to elect four other girls whom they
consider capable of carrying out the duties of guides and
counsellors or under-prefects.

"I want you to be self-governed as much as possible,
although difficulties must be brought to me, and I shall
interfere if I think it necessary. You will find the rules
of the school in each dormitory, and if you think they
are unreasonable in any way I am willing to hear what
you have to say against them.

"You have all come to Idle Pines pledged to stay a year
—unless something very unforeseen happens. At the
end of that time, if you are not happy, you may go; and
if you *are* happy, but I find that you are *not* a credit to
the school, I shall consider it my right to send you away,
for we shall follow the example of a famous old school
and take for our motto ' Either Learn or Depart.'"

"This is the 5th of May," said Wendy. "Let us give
a cheer for the girls of Idle Pines and the next 5th of
May, when I hope we shall all be the greatest of friends
and without one missing from our roll-call."

There was a rousing cheer for Idle Pines and for Miss
Wendell, and then they were all dismissed to unpack
before supper.

Pandora, who was an inmate of Sparta, in company
with four girls who were particularly desired by their
parents to be "fresh-air girls," was made indignant once
more by a remark she overheard the girl named Pauline
Miles make as they ascended the stairs.

"Mums said she was afraid this was going to be a
' crank school,' " she said to her companion, "and it jolly
well *is*—I can see that. Weren't you horribly bored by
all that ' pi-jaw ? '—elder sisters are bad enough at home,

goodness knows, without having half a dozen more at school. Did you ever see anything like that old freak in the man's boots at tea—she looks more like a great aunt than an elder sister; and as for Miss Wendell, she's right enough, of course, but I think head mistresses ought to be *frightfully* imposing. I know I used to tremble whenever Miss Abbott appeared when I first went to Hill House as a kid, but Miss Wendell looks so ordinary."

"Ordinary!" cried Pandora, "why, she's the cleverest and most original person you've ever met!"

Pauline looked Pandora up and down and said politely, "Oh, I beg your pardon; I suppose you are a *real* relative of Miss Wendell's—perhaps she is your great-aunt or something."

"No, she isn't," cried the indignant Pandora; "and she's taught us for years and years, and she's——"

"A perfect darling," said Pauline, with a giggle. "Well, we needn't fight about it. I'm sure *I* don't care, only if I like head mistresses to *look* like head mistresses, surely I can say so without having my head snapped off."

"Ugh!" said Nancy. "What a chilly place!"

"Well, there are lots of blankets," exclaimed Julie, rushing to examine the little white beds, "and it will be jollier up here at the top of the house."

"I wish I hadn't relatives who insist that the Spartan treatment is good for me," grumbled Pauline. "I *love* feather-beds and stuffy rooms, and here I am in the sort of place that would freeze a Polar explorer. I hope that Pandora girl won't sneak if we shut the windows on cold nights."

She rushed to the "Rules" hanging over the mantel-piece and began to read them.

"Well, just listen to this. Rise at six. Be in the garden school-room punctually at half-past six, wearing overalls and strong boots, ready for an hour's out-door occupa-

tion! Fancy dragging us out of bed at *six*—I call it
cruelty to animals!"

The door burst open and Eve Marriot entered in her
usual boisterous manner.

"Hallo, children! I'm to be a Spartan, too. Miss
Wendell gave me a room to share with that dreamy
die-away Penelope girl, but we should quarrel like a cat
and dog."

Before they could answer the door opened again and
Mary Ellen, very conscious of her important position as
matron, bustled in.

"Good-evening, young ladies. Dear me, not unpacked
yet and Joe coming up to move the boxes in twenty
minutes! Put your warm clothes in the bottom drawers
—that's what my mother taught me and I've never
forgotten—and the fine things on top, Miss, if you please;
and there's hooks for your dressing-gowns and dresses
in the cupboard. Now, if at any time you want anything
I'm always to be found in the old nursery down below,
and if any of you feel a *cold* about you come to me for
a hot drink and a lozenge—I can't have no colds going
through this house and Miss Rory getting it on her chest
again and all, just as she is outgrowing it."

Mary Ellen suddenly made a pounce at Julie, who had
unpacked a white satin horseshoe pincushion adorned
with yellow ribbons, which she hung over her looking-
glass.

"Are you crazy, Miss? Well, think of that now!
Hanging a horseshoe *downwards* for all your luck to
drop out of it, and who knows if one of *Them* isn't watching and ready to spite you for it!"

She seized the horseshoe and hung it with its ends
upwards, and departed with another injunction to be
quick and never dare to introduce a cold into Idle Pines.

"Well," gasped Julie, "if this isn't the rummiest school.
And who on earth is this precious Miss Rory?"

"I shouldn't like to be nursed by that person if I *do* get a cold," said Pauline. "I say, wouldn't she go for you?"

"It isn't very pleasant to hear that a person called *Them* is watching me," exclaimed Julie.

Pandora, coming up to the dormitory later to change for supper, was surprised to see how the girls had made themselves at home in Sparta.

Julie had added a fat black velvet pincushion in the shape of an owl to keep the horseshoe company, as well as a green china toad pin-tray with a gaping mouth. There was a huge yellow satin bow on her night-dress case and upon the bag that held her brushes and combs. Over Nancy's bed there was an array of photographs pinned up in the shape of a big fan, and her silver-backed brushes and combs seemed hardly suitable for a Spartan.

Pauline had photographs, too, only hers were in silver frames, and she had thrown a very elaborate blue satin eiderdown coverlet over her plain little white bed.

Eve's corner was the only unadorned one. Her dressing-gown and slippers and hair-brushes were as plain and serviceable as a boy's, and except for one photograph, "the cowboy brother," Julie said—she had nothing on her table but a row of little books on bee-keeping, gardening, cooking, etc.

Pandora was immensely interested in all these things, and she longed to know more about these schoolgirls who were to share her room. She wished they would make friends with her quickly, for she was dying to hear tales of school-life and about all the exciting things schoolgirls did in books.

She had not long to wait.

That night when the Spartans were all in bed, Julie suddenly sat up and said, "I say, Pandora, aren't you most horribly hungry?"

"*Hungry!*" Pandora turned pale with fright.

Here was a new girl complaining of starvation the very first day at school, and she would probably write home the next day and demand to be fetched away and Wendy and all of them would be ruined just as Mr. Hay had prophesied.

"Hungry," she gasped; "oh, no. You see, I had lots to eat at supper-time."

"Well, so did I"—Pandora gave a sigh of relief—"but I'm ravenous again—aren't you, girls?"

"Rather!" echoed Pauline and Nancy.

"I smuggled a whopping tin of sardines in my suit-case —I only wish I'd brought more things; that awfully rummy matron here seems as blind as a bat.

"We want bread and then we could have a topping feast. Pandora, where's the kitchen and what time does the cook go to bed?"

"It's down the back stairs," said Pan, "and Jane always goes to bed at half-past nine; she says her legs won't carry her after that."

"Lucky for us she's got crocky legs. I say, do be a sport, Pandora, and go down and forage for bread and butter while we spread out the sardines," cried Julie.

Pan hesitated. If she were to raid the larder for three hungry girls every night, Wendy would never make her fortune. At the same time it was her duty to prevent the new girls writing home and complaining of starvation.

"I'll go, of course," she said; "but wouldn't it be more exciting if we all went? There's a door at the end of this corridor leading to the back stairs and there's never anybody in the kitchen at this time of night."

The four girls donned dressing-gowns and slippers and left the dormitory on tiptoe, the moon, shining like a silver lamp through all the windows in the corridor, guiding them on their voyage of discovery.

CHAPTER 4

AN UNLUCKY ADVENTURE

"LET'S MAKE up the fire and be cosy," suggested Pauline, and immediately Pandora was seized with housewifely qualms. Schools could never become prosperous if one made raids on the coal-cellar as well as the larder, and yet she hated the girls to think her a spoil-sport.

"I don't think we'd better," she said. "You see, Jane has put the coal all ready for the morning, and if we use it up and offend her, she'll get waxy and not speak for hours and hours. Wendy says she'd rather be sent to exile in Siberia than to Coventry by Jane!"

"Well, if coals are precious we'll use wood," said Julie, and she threw on a generous log, which blazed up cheerfully; and to make things more festive Nancy lit all the candles on the mantelshelf.

"Where's the larder?" demanded Pauline.

Pandora ran to the door at the end of the kitchen and then turned round in dismay.

"It's locked!"

"Locked! what on earth for?"

"I don't know; it's *never* been before."

"Well, it's pretty polite of this Jane," cried Julie; "she evidently thinks we are all thieves."

"And we don't want anything but bread," expostulated Nancy. "I say, what luck! there's a loaf on the dresser."

"What idiots we were not to bring the sardines with us," she said; "it's much cosier here than in that windy dormitory."

"I'll go and fetch them," volunteered Pandora.

"Hush!" Julie held up her hand, and Pauline turned pale.

"What's the matter?"

"Somebody is coming down the passage. Put the light out quickly!"

Nancy blew out the candles just as the footsteps reached the door; there was a slight pause, and then the lock was turned, and the person, whoever it was, walked briskly away.

Julie flew to the door. "They've locked us in!"

"Who could it have been?" Nancy placed an eye to the dark key-hole.

As a matter of face it was Phœbe, who had been writing her weekly letter home in the maids' little sitting-room, and passing the kitchen door on her way to bed, had turned the key in the lock.

"What on earth shall we do? We can't stay here all night."

"Can't we get out another way?" The three girls looked at the miserable Pandora.

"No, the kitchen door opens into the garden and we couldn't get in through any of the windows: they are all bolted inside."

"Who comes down first?" asked Nancy.

"Tilly—she's the kitchen-maid."

"We'll get round her somehow," cried Julie. "Let's make ourselves comfortable till she comes."

Pandora dragged an old settle in front of the fire. They tried to sleep on the hard settle; but it was not a restful night. At five o'clock they all vowed they could sleep no more, and Pandora had one of her brilliant ideas.

"Wendy *loves* people to be capable," she said. "Let's get things all ready for Tilly."

"Yes; we'll light the fire," cried Julie, who had been longing to try her hand at this task ever since she entered the kitchen, and she proceeded to use up all the wood

Tilly had dried for the week, and piled a coal-scuttle of coal on the top of it.

"We might wash up all that crockery," suggested Nancy, pointing to a pile of cups and saucers in the scullery.

"I'll wash," said Nancy. "Put the kettle on, Julie; I read once that hot water and *plenty* of soap makes china shine like glass."

Nancy poured the hot water into a bowl where she had already emptied a packet of dry soap-powder, which made the cups so slippery that four of them glided out of Pandora's fingers as she dried them, and fell to the floor with a disastrous smash.

"How awful," said Pauline. "I'm jolly glad I didn't volunteer to be ' capable '."

"Well, it can't be helped," cried Nancy. "I suppose it means forking out all our pocket-money, though, to pay for them—what a beastly night it's been," and she glared at the weary Pandora, almost in tears at the sight of the wreckage before her; for it was part of the new china set chosen by Wendy and the girls for the school— a white ground with a tiny border of green pine-cones round it.

"I say, here's oatmeal or something," said Julie, who had been poking round the dresser.

"It must be for the porridge. I think I'll make it; that ought to put Tilly in a good temper."

"*Can* you make porridge?" asked Pauline scornfully.

"Of course—at least, it's just oatmeal and hot water and plenty of stirring, I suppose."

"And salt," added Nancy. "A handful of salt for each person is the Yorkshire way."

"Isn't it a handful of oatmeal and a pinch of salt for every one?" asked Pandora doubtfully.

"Well, anyhow, I'll make it," cried Julie recklessly. "Here's the pot all ready, and she emptied the whole jar of oatmeal into the pot and set it over a fierce fire, adding enough salt to make the inmates of Idle Pines thirsty for a week.

She stirred it conscientiously till it came to a boil, then at Pauline's command from the window to come and see "the great-aunt in the man's boots," she flew with the others to enjoy the spectacle of Miss Billock trundling a huge wheel-barrow towards the kitchen-garden, the ridiculously small hat still perched upon her forehead.

"Isn't she absurd?" said Julie.

"I shall call her Aunt Sally," promised Pauline. "That idiotic little hat ought to be knocked off like a coconut," and Julie and Nancy hailed Miss Billock's nick-name with delight.

"What an awful smell!" sniffed Nancy. Julie flew to her porridge-pot, but it was too late: a thick sticky stream was bubbling over the stove, and the bottom of the pan was crackling with burn.

"There now!" cried Julie in dismay, while Pandora sighed with despair. "We've done it now, and it's all through Aunt Sally; there's not much hope for us *now* with a mess like this."

"And somebody's coming," whispered Nancy, and in another second Tilly entered the kitchen.

Staring round her in amazement, she seemed to take in the situation at a glance, and her face became scarlet with wrath.

"So this is the sort of thing I've got to put up with in a *young ladies'* school, is it, Miss Pandora? What *you* call ' 'aving a bit of fun,' I expect, and then off you go and leave *me* to clean up all this muck!

"You think you'll get round me, I suppose, not to let on. Not me; I'm going to Miss Wendell the moment I've put on the kettle for that there Madam's early tea and not a word you say will stop me!"

"Come along," said Pandora hastily, and she dragged the girls away.

"Where are you going?" asked Julie.

"To tell Wendy myself, of course," replied Pandora, and she suddenly opened a door and made them all visible to their head mistress, who was up early as usual and busy at her writing-table.

"Pandora! Why are you not in the garden with the others?"

"Because we went down last night to get bread for a midnight feast of sardines, and somebody locked us in the kitchen, and we've been there all night. So this morning we thought we'd be useful"—the four girls all tried to look tired and virtuous—"and we've broken four cups and burnt the porridge, and Tilly is simply furious."

Miss Wendell looked at them all shrewdly, then she remarked quietly: "Poor children—how ugly you look."

"*Ugly!*" Pauline gasped. She had been told she looked pretty scores of times, and neither Nancy, Pandora, nor Julie considered herself plain.

"Yes; yellow faces and rings round one's eyes always look ugly, and I suppose it's rich sardines at midnight after an ample supper of cocoa and sandwiches, that have made your noses so red—indigestion, you know. It seems to me a stupid thing to prefer sardines to dreams, too, and I thought you were interesting girls. Go upstairs and have a bath and then go to Dorothy—she is in the garden—and tell her I want her to ' tone you up,' as you have all had a *bad* night. We'll talk about disobedience, burnt porridge, and broken cups after prayers. Shut the door, please." And Wendy went calmly on with her writing.

Once outside the door Julie gasped, "Well—Miss Abbott would have jawed for hours and hours, and then sent us off to bed."

When the bath was over, and, attired in the short brown skirts and loose cream silk jumpers with wide-open collars and short sleeves prescribed by Wendy for everyday wear at Idle Pines, the four girls refreshed themselves with the milk and brown rolls they found in the hall, and then went to deliver Wendy's message to Miss Dorothy Rew.

"Well, you *do* look frightful," was her unflattering comment. You had better get some of this glorious air inside you at once," and she proceeded to instruct them in a new breathing-exercise which "toned-up" Pauline a little more than she enjoyed.

"That will do," ordered Dorothy, after ten minutes of this treatment. "Pauline is turning green—shows she breathes all wrong. Do you see that little hut among the gorse? It's full of bundles of pea-sticks, which Miss Billock wants for staking the young peas. You can carry a lot into the kitchen-garden before breakfast," and Dorothy strolled away.

"Pretty cool, to turn us into gardener's boys," grumbled Pauline.

There were girls everywhere, dressed in green linen overalls and wearing sturdy shoes and shady hats. Penelope and Cassandra were instructing Eve in milking, and Aurora, an efficient stable-woman since babyhood, was helping to groom the ponies, scrambling between their legs in a way she hoped would make the scornful Meg Connell envious.

There were girls mowing and girls rolling the tennis and croquet-lawns. A little group was weeding the strawberry-beds, and another was gathered round Miss Billock in the potting-shed, while she loudly lectured them on the right and wrong way of handling a young seedling.

At eight o'clock, when overalls and thick shoes were discarded, every one was ravenous for the breakfast they had helped to carry out and lay on the long tables on the veranda

Unlimited porridge and new milk, bread and butter and marmalade and hot coffee tasted delicious out in the May sunshine.

"Lots of people would have made us eat the burnt porridge," whispered Nancy, "and I must say I expected it."

"Wendy wouldn't," said Pan, "but she'll punish us in a way that makes us feel horribly small and greedy, you'll see."

Prayers over, they presented themselves to Wendy.

"Well, girls," she began, "I have come to the conclusion that you are all suffering from two things—indigestion and stupidity. Dyspeptic people always have a desire for rich food at wrong times—sardines at midnight, for instance, and surely only stupid people would bring punishments and impositions upon themselves by breaking a rule in order to have a rather dull and unoriginal adventure, when there are so many amusing things to do in this place, where I am trying to give you as much liberty as possible. I am very vexed, because I dislike worrying my brain with thinking of punishments—I would rather use it for something more useful to you and myself. But if you *will* break the few rules I have made, I certainly shall punish you severely, for though I wish you to be free and happy at Idle Pines, I do not intend you to be undisciplined.

"Now, exercise is good for indigestion—Dorothy will give you some suitable ones from six-thirty to seven every morning, and again in the evening recreation hour, for the next fortnight. At seven you will go to Jane in the kitchen and learn from her the art of porridge-making.

"Tilly fetched me to see the mess *you* call porridge,

and I confess I was shocked that four girls of fourteen or thereabouts should themselves be so incapable.

"When Jane has taught you, I want all four of you to take turns in making the morning porridge for the whole school for a fortnight."

She smiled whimsically. "To-day, too, I should like you to wash up all the tea-things—Jane will explain to you why it is that cups sometimes behave as eels. As you have broken four of my new ones, I'm afraid you must use mugs until we can match them. At the end of the fortnight, I shall ask you to give a demonstration on porridge-making to the whole school in the little laundry. Now run away and try to be sensible children for the future."

"How small she makes you feel," said Nancy, when they were outside the door.

"Wendy always can," said Pandora, who was miserable because Wendy had ignored her pathetic, silent appeals for forgiveness.

"I feel such a greedy little horror, too," groaned Julie.

"I call it an absurd fuss about nothing," grumbled Pauline.

Madame Clément swept by her on her way to the schoolroom.

"*Mes enfants!*" she said sweetly. "Mademoiselle has just told me that you have a verra, verra great interest in the sardines, *n'est ce pas?* Come to me at three this afternoon, and I will speak with you of those who catch these little fish on our coast so beautiful of Brittany. Afterwards we will make a little French composition—*hein?*" and, smiling still more sweetly, she passed on her way.

CHAPTER 5

PRINCESS CHARMING ARRIVES

THE next day Jill arrived, and from the very moment she stepped out of the pony-cart which brought her from the station, Pandora and Aurora were the admirers and slaves of this Princess Charming.

She was not only ravishingly pretty, but she had an exciting sort of presence, and one felt instantly that she had seen things and done things much more thrilling than creeping downstairs for a midnight feast of sardines. Even her luggage was covered all over with foreign labels, and the clothes she wore on arrival, to quote Madame Clément, were perhaps a little too *chic* for a schoolgirl. She was very tall and slender, and her perfect little oval face was framed in short, silky black hair which curled round just the sort of ears a heroine should have, ears like little shells, as delicately coloured as her cheeks. Her eyes were of the deepest violet, and her nose was "tip-tilted." Her mouth was demure, and when she laughed she showed two rows of pearls just as a heroine should. She had charming manners, too, for when Miss Billock—now referred to by all the junior girls as "Aunt Sally"—came in to tea with a great deal of garden mould on her boots, and a very large bunch of radishes to eat with her bread and butter, she did not look in the least surprised, but passed her the bread as though she were a most elegant guest.

She made friends at once, and before she had been at Idle Pines an hour she was seated in the little round summer-house—it was the recreation hour—surrounded by an admiring crowd of juniors. She looked like a gay little coloured butterfly amidst brown moths, for she had not yet donned the school-dress, and her short rose-coloured linen skirts, and big shady hat with just one silky rose on the brim, made her look astonishingly pretty.

She at once produced a large white packet of chocolate caramels tied with rose-coloured ribbons, and passed them round generously.

"We aren't supposed to eat sweets before supper," said Meg Connell, who was not only inclined to be a little priggish, but a little jealous too, for she had undoubtedly been the prettiest girl in the school until Jill arrived.

"Well, you needn't," said Aurora, still smarting under Meg's snubs, and she passed over Meg when the bag came near her.

"But I have not read the Rules of the school yet," exclaimed Jill; "and as you all look like Brownies or Girl Guides or something of that sort, I suppose it is your duty to prevent casualties in the school camp."

"What on earth do you mean?" asked Julie.

"Well, you see, if you don't help me to eat this stuff, I shall have to eat it all myself—I'm a pig about chocolate caramels—and if I do I shall be horribly ill, so it is your duty to help me."

"Oh, of course, if it's to prevent a school-fellow suffering, I suppose we *can* break rules," said Julie, with a grin, and, encouraged by her example, every one munched caramels except Meg, who regarded Rory furiously.

"Have you ever been to school before?" Pandora asked Jill.

"Been to school before!" Jill threw up her hands with a gesture remarkably like Madame Clément's when amazed at a pupil's ignorance. "My child, I've been to *millions* of schools."

"You shouldn't tell stories," said Meg, still prim;

"how could a girl of your age have been to *millions* of schools?"

Jill surveyed her so steadily that Meg became uncomfortably scarlet. Then the new girl said sadly:

"Why don't you like me?"

"I never said I didn't."

"No, but you *look* it; and you won't break bread with me—I mean munch caramels. I can't bear people not to like me, so do have one and stop snubbing me, *please*," and Jill offered the caramels with such an enchanting smile that Meg obligingly took three to make up for those she had missed.

"Do tell us about them," cried Pandora.

"The schools—my dear, it would take me hundreds of years to describe them; you see, Moti is mad——"

"Who is Moti?"

"She's my mother."

"Your *mother*—and she's *mad*. How *awful*!" gasped Pauline.

"She's only school-mad; you see——"

"But why don't you call her Mother?" asked Nancy.

"She doesn't like it. She says she'll never be a mother nor a grandmother, nor an aunt, it sounds so old and she feels so young—every one thinks she's my sister."

"But what does Moti mean?" demanded Aurora, feeling the new girl and her relations grew more interesting every moment.

"It means 'Pearl' in Hindustani, and Dad always calls her that, and so did I when I was a kid in India. Her real name is Marguerite, but Moti suits her better and she loves it."

"And is she really mad?" asked Pauline, rather hoping she was.

"Mad on schools. You see, I'm the only one, and rather precious to Moti, and she's terrified she won't do her duty by me; so she tries every fresh school she hears about, hoping it will be the one to make me into some-thing really perfect."

"And why did you leave them?"

"Because I didn't become perfect—I only got colds and backaches and wrong ideas, Moti says. When I first came from India I was most frightfully delicate, and she sent me to a home school kept by two ladies who were supposed to look after you. They wrapped me up in prickly flannel, rubbed the skin off my chest until it was raw, and shut me up in such stuffy rooms that I caught pneumonia every time I went out. So Moti fetched me away, and as the Doctor said I must have lots of fresh air and plenty of liberty, I went to a school where the windows were never shut, and where you wore the same clothes in the winter as you did in the summer, and none at all sometimes. You see, they were mad on sun-baths, and used to stick us on the lawn to bask, until one poor atom got a sunstroke through the sun being too hot on her spine or something. Then Moti got an awful fright and rushed to fetch me away, and got me a governess instead; but *she* didn't do either."

"Why?" The girls listened breathlessly.

"Moti was so mad on fresh air just then that she made me have all my lessons and all my meals out of doors, and Miss Bell hated it—she said the wind made her feel as though she must scream, and she left and I went to an ordinary school. It was all rules and bells and lessons, and we walked out like a Noah's Ark procession. Moti said it was stifling me and she couldn't stand having a daughter cut out of one pattern like a thousand other people's daughters, so she sent me to a vegetarian school where I got indigestion. Then I went to one where there were no rules——"

"No *rules*!"

"No; you just worked when you felt inclined—they didn't believe in forcing the intelligence. I was fright-

P.C.   D

fully careful with mine"—she gave an impish smile—
"and if you did awful things the head mistress led you
into a room and begged you most kindly to tell her just
what was on your mind when you did them, to get at
what she called the psychological reason—or some such
rot—for you being a silly ass. We wore breeches and did
the rummiest exercises when we ought to have been in
bed and asleep, Moti said, and I left because she said she'd
rather have a child that could do nothing but fancy-work
and giggle, than an 'undisciplined crank.' Then we
heard of Idle Pines, and Moti said, 'I believe this is *It* at
last, ducksie'—and it is just at the right time, too,
because she had to go back to India and Dad—so here
I am."

"Shall you stay at school for the hols.?" asked Pauline.
"How rotten!"

"Of course I shall."

"And so shall I," announced Aurora.

"How nice," said Jill, and she said it in a way that
made Rory more adoring than ever, for Jill was an
important person of fourteen, and Rory had been snubbed
by her elders more than she liked during the last twenty-
four hours.

"Where are you going to sleep?" inquired Pauline.

"In the dormitory with the poppies crawling everywhere."

"They're not crawling," cried Pan indignantly.

"I wish you were sleeping in Sparta," said Julie, who
had come to the conclusion that the new girl was amusing; "it's at the top of the house and we can have lots of
fun."

"Oh, lots!" said Pauline bitterly, who had two fingers
burnt with porridge-making and a French composition
on sardine-fishing in Brittany returned on her hands by
Madame Clément with "*Très mauvais. Recrivez, s'il vous
plait*" written across it.

"Well, I *shall* sleep there soon," announced Jill.

"But you can't, if you're in ' Somnus.'"

"Yes, I can; you see, I've got the artistic temperament. I've heard Moti tell people that scores of times, and that means you're a person that can't stand poppies crawling over curtains and things for too long. When they begin to make me feel that I must scream, I shall write and tell Moti that ' Somnus' gives me insomnia, and ask her to let Miss Wendell put me into that jolly dormitory with the gods and goddesses flying over the walls, and when I'm sick of gods and goddesses, I shall write to Moti again and tell her to ask Miss Wendell to put me in ' Sparta,' because flying gods and goddesses on the wall make me dream."

"And if you don't like ' Sparta '?" asked Pandora anxiously.

"My artistic temperament might have to have a room to itself—you never can tell! But I don't think it will," said Jill thoughtfully, "because, you see, I'm one of those persons who simply can't believe there isn't a ghost behind the bed, and a burglar under it when I sleep alone. Besides, it would be dangerous."

"*Dangerous!*"

"Yes, because I walk in my sleep sometimes."

"Walk in your sleep! How awful!" shuddered Pauline, hoping Jill wouldn't want to scream at poppies and flying gods for ages and ages.

"*Do* you mean like the man who got up and watered all the streets, and the people who get up and sweep the house and cook the dinner and don't remember a thing about it in the morning?" asked Rory.

"I never water streets, nor clean houses," said Jill; "but once I got up and painted a row of black cats on the new wallpaper in the drawing-room—cream, you know, just the place for black cats—and Moti *wouldn't* let me; but, of course, asleep I wasn't responsible for my actions and it would have been dangerous to wake me."

"What shall we do if you walk to-night?" asked a sleeper in "Somnus" anxiously.

"Follow me, of course—even if I go over the cliffs and into the sea for a moonlight bathe, you must follow me and see I don't drown. But don't wake me—you must *never* wake a sleep-walker—I mean a somnambulist; and if you do I shall have a fit and die and you'll all be imprisoned for manslaughter."

Much as Aurora admired the new-comer, she began to regret that her bed was next to hers, for she was a sleepy little person, and it was not very pleasant to have to keep awake on purpose to watch that Jill didn't drown herself.

Before Jill could relate any more thrilling details of her past life, Mary Leslie appeared and said crossly, "Why on earth are you all chattering like monkeys here? Laurette told you to be under the cedar at half-past six to discuss the Rules. And let me tell you at once, I don't intend to follow you about like an old hen after her chicks: come at once."

Wendy had elected Penelope, and a girl named Laurette Page, as prefects, though Pen had objected strongly, as, to tell the truth, she felt a little alarmed at the thought of acting as counsellor to a crowd of critical schoolgirls. But Wendy had insisted. Laurette didn't mind in the least; she had been next to the head girl at Hill House, and she was not afraid of snubbing fifty juniors if they needed it; but she was not quite sure if she approved of all the liberty Miss Wendell allowed them. It was she who really presided over the council under the great cedar tree on the west lawn.

"We are here, girls," she began, after scolding them for being late, "to discuss the Rules of the school. You heard what Miss Wendell said the other evening, that if we found any of them unreasonable she would be willing to consider our objection. For my part—and I am sure Penelope feels the same——"

Pen woke up with a start, and thinking they were still talking about unpunctuality said, in the most school-marmy way she could adopt, "Yes, I think it is *frightfully* rude to keep people waiting." Laurette surveyed her pityingly and continued—"For my part I think them most reasonable, but you all have a say in the matter, so if you have any grievance let us hear it at once."

"Well, I think we've got a grievance about getting up at six o'clock," said Pauline. "It's only five really, and beastly chilly this morning; besides, I've felt yawny all day."

"A person who sits up all night usually yawns all day," answered Laurette pointedly. "Perhaps you'd like me to interview Miss Wendell and tell her we all consider we ought to have an early cup of tea at seven, before rising? Don't waste time by being stupid, please; Miss Wendell would never think of re-considering the whole time-table because one person is lazy."

"Mr. Chairman—ladies. I should be glad if you will lend me your ears while I state my grievance." Jill in her rose-coloured skirts and flowery hat stood up in the midst of the company.

"What is it?" demanded Laurette.

"It is this, Mr. Chairman. I am called to attend this meeting and am nearly blown-up for not knowing I was expected—to give my valuable time to a question I have not yet had an opportunity of studying carefully. In other words, I have not yet seen the Rules of Idle Pines."

"Well, whose fault is that? There is a copy in every dormitory and one in each class-room," cried Laurette. "*Why* haven't you seen them, may I ask?"

"Because since my arrival I have had only time to take the sustenance necessary after a long journey, and since then I have been discussing the rules of other schools with my friends and comrades," answered Jill primly, with a demure smile at the others.

"Don't be absurd, please. I have a copy here, so you can read them now," and Laurette, who was dying to play tennis, passed a list of the school Rules to Jill and tried to restrain her impatience while the new girl studied them with devout interest.

"Oh, do be quick," she called out at last, and Jill turned slowly round.

"Well?"

"Mr. Chairman—ladies. After carefully perusing the paper before me I have come to the conclusion that Rule IV is unreasonable, and will cause annoyance and inconvenience to most of us."

"Read it out."

"Rule IV," read Jill. "No pupil is allowed to spend even the smallest amount of her pocket-money without the consent of a prefect."

"Well, I don't see any hardship in that," cried Laurette.

"And if you want to know why Miss Wendell made that Rule I'll tell you," said Cassandra. "It is because the village is within bounds, and if you all go there you'll spend your money on those disgusting sweets at the village shop, and get pains and be a bother to everybody."

"But I never eat disgusting sweets," replied Jill, with an aristocratic shudder. "And I don't want to have to give an account of how I spend my Saturday penny."

"Well, you'll have to, as nobody else has complained about the Rule, and it is a reasonable one."

"Suppose we want to buy the prefects a little present as a surprise," said Jill sweetly; "something to show our love and appreciation of them, you know—not disgusting sweets, of course."

"Don't talk nonsense, please; you can surprise and please us now by being quick. Now, does anybody else share this grievance? If so, hands up."

Several more hands went up, and Jill smiled amiably. Personally she didn't care a straw about asking permission to spend her pocket-money, and possessed none at the moment, as she had recklessly given it all away to a blind man with "a most darling dog" in Southampton Station; but she considered the meeting dull, and immediately tried to bring a little liveliness into the proceedings.

"Well, you had better all give me your names, and I'll tell Miss Wendell you object to Rule IV," said Laurette crossly, and ten of Jill's admirers instantly entered their names and Laurette dismissed the meeting and Penelope came back to the world with a start.

Mary Ellen pounced on Jill as she crossed the lawn.

"You'll please come upstairs, Miss, and I'll help you to arrange your clothes before supper; you seem to have quite a bride's trowsoo," she added disapprovingly.

The much belabelled box was certainly fitted with things not usually found among schoolgirl luggage, dainty garments and luxuries bestowed by Jill's impulsive mother as farewell gifts to her most precious child. There was a crocodile dressing-case, filled with ivory-backed brushes and combs, and little ivory boxes with the monogram M. B. on them all in silver, for Jill's real name was Marguerite Beville, too. There were silver-topped bottles of delicious scent, embroidered bags, a diamond brooch, a turquoise necklace and bracelets, and a night-dress case of fine Brussels lace. Jill's dressing-gown and slippers were of rose-coloured silk, and the amount of dainty underclothes and white summer frocks she possessed could not be squeezed into the drawers allotted to each girl in "Somnus."

"You'll never want all these petticoats; they'll have to go in my cupboard," said Mary Ellen, examining the fine lace on them with respect. "Goodness me, what's this, Miss?"

She held out a bright green silk frock, extremely scanty and short.

"That's the dress I sometimes wore at the dancing-class; there's a petticoat to match it somewhere."

"Graham and green should ne'er be seen," quoted Mary Ellen. "And it is not only folk named Graham that shouldn't put a green dress on their backs—those that do it never get any peace from *Them*, Miss, you mark my words."

"Who on earth are *Them*?"

Mary Ellen looked shocked. Rory would have known at once to whom she referred.

"The Little People, Miss. Green's the colour that rightly belongs to the trees and the grass and the little folk that lives among them, and human beings didn't ought to offend the creatures by making their own dresses of it. My cousin's daughter—a fine bonny girl she was—would have a green dress one Whit Sunday when I was a little one up in Wales. She was lying in the churchyard before next Whitsun. A decline the doctor called it, but it was nothing but all the worriting the fairy folk gave her."

"Well, perhaps that's why I'm so unlucky," said Jill dolefully, and her mouth suddenly quivered. "There's Moti gone away for a whole year, and I believe I'm going into a decline like your cousin's daughter with the green dress—my head aches frightfully and so does my back."

She flung herself down on the bed, and her little oval face grew suddenly pale and pinched.

Mary Ellen surveyed her carefully, and never said a word about the crushed counterpane, for though she would talk for hours on fairy lore, she was a sensible, shrewd, kind woman, or Miss Wendell would never have put her to watch over thirty careless school-girls.

"This is one of the delicate ones, like Miss Rory," she thought rapidly. "Bubbling up like fizzy stuff one minute, and then going all flat and weepy;" and she put away the green dress and said firmly, "Not you, Miss, you're all wore out with the journey and everything a bit strange like. Now, you get into bed, dearie, and you shall have your supper on a tray, and a nap before those noisy girls come to bed."

"I don't want any supper," said Jill; "besides, what would Miss Wendell say?"

"She won't say nothing, Miss," said Mary Ellen with dignity. "If I think you're better quiet in bed that's enough for her. 'You look after their stomachs and I'll look after their brains,' she says to me. And it's your stomach that's making you feel so poorly—trains are nasty things."

While she talked she brushed out Jill's silky hair.

"There, you'll feel as right as ninepence in the morning," she said. "Would you like Miss Rory to bring your supper to you?"

"Which is Rory—that darling person like an elf?"

"She's the prettiest of the bunch, Miss," said Mary Ellen with pride. "And the little heart in her is made with gold—except when she's 'fairy taken,' then she's a rare handful."

"Please let her come, and thanks most awfully for being such a duck to me," and Jill touched Mary Ellen's rosy country cheeks with a butterfly kiss before she bustled away to get her a hot-water bottle. This she tucked under her feet and left her to herself.

Warmed and comforted she lay in bed gazing through the open window.

"I believe Moti is right," she murmured, "and this is *It* at last. What a jolly place it is and who ever heard of a matron named Mary Ellen who believes in fairies. Now Jill, my child, remember this is a nice school, and when you feel you are going to do something outrageous you've got to stop it——"

The door opened softly and Rory appeared, carefully carrying a little blue-painted tray containing a deep yellow bowl full of hot creamy bread and milk.

She put it down before Jill and said triumphantly, "I made Mary Ellen give you one of the yellow bowls —we always have them when we are ill: even if you feel sick and don't want anything, you eat it because it's such fun to find out what's at the bottom of the bowl."

Not in the least hungry, but curious, Jill took the spoon and ate steadily, while Rory perched on the bed.

"It's the Blue Bird one!" Rory cried joyfully, as Jill took her last spoonful and regarded with pleasant excitement a fat blue bird swinging on a bunch of cherry blossom, at the bottom of her bowl.

"What luck!—Blue Bird for Happiness—and you'll be happy here. You see, Mary Ellen always shuts her eyes when she chooses a bowl, so we *never* know until the last mouthful."

Jill, feeling better already after the warm milk, admired the Blue Bird that was to bring her happiness at Idle Pines, and said, "I believe I'll get up now and go out and explore that wood."

"But you *mustn't*!" cried Rory in alarm.

"Is it a wood—I mean a proper wood, with moss pincushions and trees twisted like old witches, and bats, and primroses and rabbits?" asked Jill.

"It's the Glen," said Rory; "and hardly anybody goes there except us at this time of the year. The rabbits play hide-and-seek in the moonlight there—Pan and I have seen them scores of times; and there are squirrels, too, and crowds of primroses, and it's knee-deep in bluebells; and later there'll be the darlingest toad-stools, all yellow and brown and scarlet and cream, growing round the pine-trees in rings. Mary Ellen says——"

Rory stopped suddenly. She had been snubbed so often by girls of Jill's age during the last two days that she felt afraid Jill would be bored with her too.

"What does she say?"

"If I tell, you'll say I'm a kid—just like that Meg girl. But I don't care: Pandora's *fourteen* and she believes they're there too."

Jill sat up in bed and said, "I don't care if you *are* a kid —kids are *much* nicer than goats, and if that Meg doesn't be careful she'll grow up into a nasty, disagreeable nanny-goat before she's had any fun. *Do* tell me what Mary Ellen says are in the wood besides primroses and rabbits—or shall I guess?"

"Oh, do; but I don't believe you can."

"Yes, I can: listen—it's *Them*."

Jill's face was perfectly serious, and Rory glowed with happiness; here at last was a person who understood.

"Yes; how *did* you know?"

"It looks a wood like that—all quiet and deep and murmury—not a tame place with notice-boards and a path down the middle."

She lay down again, and Rory surveyed her anxiously.

"Do you think you will walk in your sleep to-night?"

A glint of mischief appeared in Jill's eyes, and she said guardedly, "I don't know; I might—and I mightn't."

Aurora sighed, and Jill added, "I hope I don't, because it makes my legs ache, and I want to do something most awfully, early to-morrow morning."

"Oh, what?" asked Rory.

"Get up at dawn"—alas for Jill's good intentions— "and go and lose something in that wood."

"*Lose* something!"

"Yes, a green silk dress; will you come, too?"

Totally forgetting that she was now a schoolgirl, she said, "I should just rather think I will!"

CHAPTER 6

AURORA, THE DAWN-MAIDEN

EVERYBODY else was sleeping soundly when Aurora poked Jill gently, and she opened her eyes.

"It's time," murmured Rory, and Jill stretched luxuriously—she was not so keen on early rising as she had been the night before, and was not sure if she didn't think "kids" of Rory's age a nuisance after all.

"Never mind, if you are too sleepy," whispered Rory sadly, and Jill suddenly sat up in bed and cried, "But I'm not sleepy, and I'm dying to come."

"Hush!" said Rory; "we'll carry our clothes to the bathroom and dress there. If we let the water run on to our sponges, nobody can hear. Pan and I always do."

Washing and dressing, was accomplished noiselessly.

"We must go down the back stairs," said Rory. "The dogs are in the hall, and they'll go mad if they think we're going out."

"Let's take them," suggested Jill; "they're such ducks."

"They are angels; but we can't. You see, when they get into the Glen they *will* go down rabbit-holes and we should never get them home again. We'll take Satan, though," and Rory softly opened the kitchen door, and Satan, always waiting for a great adventure, marched out, his black plumy tail waving erect.

Rory turned the key of the door, and they both stepped into the garden.

"Shut your eyes, and don't open them till I say 'Now'," commanded Rory, taking hold of Jill's arm when they reached the end of the path, and Jill obediently became blind.

"Now!" called out Rory, when she and Jill and the galloping Satan had at last reached the spot with which she wished to impress her guest; "now—is it a *real* wood?"

For a moment Jill did not speak, for the wood was not only real, but the wood of her dreams. The dark pines, quiet and tall sentinels round the oaks, rising like kings wearing amber-gold crowns, the ground beneath them with its covering of scented pine-needles and the wood-anemones, pale and beautiful. Rabbits, waving their little white flags, scuttled into their burrows; a little stream sang and murmured silvery songs over grey, mossy stones, and the great elm-tree fallen across it was covered with ferns more delicate and lovely than a wood-nymph's hair.

"Now, shut your eyes again," ordered Rory, satisfied with Jill's silent understanding of a "real" wood, and she led her on again until she was giddy, and after a short climb cried, "Now!" once more.

The pines were all gone and the stream had suddenly found its way across yellow sands into deep, deep blue sea. Below them the Glen lay in a green cup, its sides covered with primroses, golden gorse bushes and baby birch trees like maidens shaking their silvery tresses over the singing stream. At the bottom of the cup there lay a lake of bluebells, bluer than the sea, bluer than heaven, bluer than anything Jill had ever seen in her life.

"Oh, how perfectly, perfectly lovely!" she gasped.

"Do you see that little green knoll just where the pine-trees stop, where the wild apple-blossom has fallen?" asked Rory with excitement.

"Yes."

"Well, that's where *They* are; it's where we find the rings, you know, and once Pan found nine hazel leaves in a sort of circle."

"What a darling place; and if there *are* a *Them*, just the place for them," cried Jill. "Now, let's go and lay the green dress on the knoll as a peace-offering and then go down there and pick millions and millions of blue-bells."

"I shall have to catch Satan first," said Rory. "He always *will* go down the rabbit-holes at the back of the knoll, and I'm terrified *They* will carry him off."

She caught the big, black purring cat leaping after the sulphur-coloured butterflies that fluttered above the bluebells, and hugged him firmly as they climbed up to the knoll.

"Most wonderful and beautiful Little Persons," chanted Jill, arranging the silken folds of the green dress at the top of the knoll, "here is the green dress to keep and wrap round your lovely fairy forms; and forgive me for ever putting your very own colour on to my own clumsy human one—I never knew 'I didn't ought to have done it' until Mary Ellen told me. And please don't punish me and 'worrit' me to death, nor give me a green eye and a blue one; and please, *please* don't put a changeling into my bed instead of me, because Moti rather likes me as I am and changelings are such horrid persons."

Jill never smiled as she made this speech, in fact she looked so solemn that Rory hugged herself and Satan with joy; for to be in a wood just after dawn with a girl who made an offering to the fairies thrilled her imagina-tion, as she really believed in the Little People as firmly as did her old nurse, and to her every tree and flower in the Glen was haunted by the fairy folk.

"And now," said Jill, "we'll pick bluebells."

"Mary Ellen says," related Rory, "that if you give *Them* a gift and they like it, they *always* give you one too. Wouldn't it be gorgeous if they did?—to find it in the bluebells, you know—a little wishing-cap or something like that?"

"Gorgeous!" murmured Jill.

"And if you find a *white* bluebell, Mary Ellen says it's a sign that *They* are not very far away," chattered on Rory. "Oh, look! There *is* a white one over there with enormous bells—they ring white bells for the christening of the fairy babies, you know."

"Listen! what on earth's that?" asked Jill, suddenly standing still.

"It's something crying," said Rory. "Oh, Jill, suppose it's a rabbit caught in a trap!"

"Then the sooner we get there the better," cried Jill, and she ran towards the sound, followed by Rory.

The bluebells grew very tall and thick at the foot of a small pine tree, and as they ran towards it Jill suddenly tripped over the end of a bright green shawl, and Rory clutched her at the same moment.

"Oh, look!" she whispered; "*it's a baby!*"

A baby it was, now fast asleep again among the blue-bells, the folds of the green shawl tucked round its chubby little limbs.

"Where on earth did it come from?" asked Jill.

"Oh, Jill, don't you know?" cried Rory, awestruck. "Look! there's the white bluebell growing at the very edge of the shawl; it's a gift from *Them*, of course."

"But we don't want it," exclaimed Jill.

"Not *want* it?" Rory surveyed her with horror.

"It *must* belong to somebody," cried Jill.

"No, it doesn't. Who would leave a baby lying in a wood all by itself to be carried off to an eagle's nest, or to be stolen by gipsies?"

"But there aren't any eagles."

"There *might* be," said Rory mysteriously, "and there are lots and lots of gipsies in the Forest—they might come here any moment to pick bluebells to sell."

"Well, if anybody has put it down here they don't deserve to find it again," said Jill, "and it *would* be fun to have a baby of one's own."

"But where on earth shall we put it? You smuggle a baby into a dormitory as you can a dor or a guinea-pig."

"We could keep it in the Sanctuary," cried Rory.

"What's that?"

"It's a secret. You see, Pandora and I have both got our birthdays on the same day—July 20th—though we're not twins. Mary Ellen calls it a coin-*ci*-dence, and Father used to say it was an economy, because we could both have the same treat.

"When we were little we wanted a tiny house in the wood more than anything else, and when Father found it out he sent us away with Wendy for two weeks, and we came back on our birthday, and there was the house all built—our very, very own, and the land it stands on, too. Nobody can take it away without our consent, nor even walk inside the house unless we say so."

"How perfectly ravishing!"

"We were awfully sorry for Pen and Cassandra, because they loved it too, so we arranged to give them ' sanctuary '—you know that jolly old thing they did in the olden times when people ran away from the law —Cassandra could fly there when Mary Ellen wanted to wash her hair, and she didn't want to be bothered because she was writing a poem; and Pen came when she wanted to just sit and do nothing and Wendy wouldn't let her; and even Father took sanctuary, too, when he wanted to read Greek, and Mr. Hay called and would talk about business. Mary Ellen used to be furious, and Wendy was angry, too, sometimes; but Father said they must respect sanctuary law, and if they could only get there they were safe, only sometimes Mary Ellen and Wendy and Mr. Hay caught them long before they did."

"And is it there still?"

"Of course; and though Wendy said if we had a school we must share the ponies, and not mind if the girls turned the angels off the veranda chairs she *never* said we must share the Sanctuary, because Father gave it to us —though, of course, we shall let our very *dearest* friends come in," and Rory gave Jill a delicious smile.

"Where is it?"

"It's in our own little pine-wood by the orchard. We could put the baby there, and nobody would hear it if it cried, and we could take it in turns to mind it. Oh, *what* a pity we didn't find it before we had a school! There was such loads more time then," lamented Rory.

"Well, if it wasn't a school I shouldn't be here to give my green dress to *Them*, and, according to you, there wouldn't have been any baby then," remarked Jill. "I say, it's waking up! I wonder what colour its eyes are?"

The baby kicked the folds of the shawl from its chubby limbs, crumpled up two delicious fists and opened eyes —not the fairy blue of the flowers that cradled it, but as black and velvety as sloes in autumn-time.

It was a baby girl, and its fat little limbs were clad in a single cotton garment under the bright green shawl. It never cried, even when Satan pounced on an imaginary field-mouse under the fringe of the shawl, but stared up in baby wonder at the two girls, and then gave a delicious gurgle.

"*Isn't* it a lovely duck?" cried Jill, and Rory hung over it in rapture.

"It oughtn't to be uncovered in the morning dew," said Jill, and she seized the baby and cuddled it to her so long that Rory asked plaintively, "Oughtn't twin mothers to hold a baby in turns?"

"Well, don't drop her, for goodness' sake!" cried Jill, putting the bundle into Rory's arms reluctantly.

"Let's take her up to the Sanctuary before anybody is about," suggested Rory. "No, Satan, you must walk, and don't go rabbiting, for goodness' sake, while I've got my hands full of this precious child!"

"I'll take her," said Jill, longing for her turn again, but Rory staggered on until she tripped over the end of the green shawl and fell headlong in the bluebells with her burden.

"There! I told you so!" cried Jill, seizing the baby, who gave a yell. "We'll have to take her to a specialist now to see if her spine is injured."

Consoled with the promise that she should have her turn when they reached safety in the Sanctuary, Rory captured Satan and led the way up a woodland path which was a short cut to their own little pinewood, followed by Jill and the baby, now contentedly cooing once more.

"Here we are," announced Rory at last.

"I don't see anything."

"No, that's the lovely part of it," and Rory plunged between gorse bushes as golden as the sun and as high as a cottage, leading to a clearing in the wood, and Jill, panting a little, for the baby was fat, cried, "Oh, how perfectly lovely!"

In front of them were four pine-trees, and built between them, of pine-logs, was a round house with a thatched roof. The window-panes and door were painted green, and in the middle of the door there swung an old copper knocker—the head of Pan, the woodland god, holding a round copper ring between his grinning lips.

"Once hold on to the ring and you're safe," explained Rory, and she disappeared mysteriously behind the Sanctuary, returning in a moment with a key, with which she unlocked the door, and then invited Jill to enter.

Never was there such a charming house except in a

fairy tale! The kitchen floor was wooden, and scrubbed to snowy whiteness, and there was a tiny range covered with shining pots and pans, with an oven large enough to cook for quite a number of refugees flying from tiresome Mary Ellens and visitors.

There was a dresser in the corner holding green cups and saucers and plates, a corner cupboard, a table covered with a cloth embroidered with green, and the cushions on the low wooden chairs and the curtains at the window were of green chintz with a pattern of pine-cones upon it.

Jill tucked up the baby on one of the chairs, and Rory was in the seventh heaven of rapture, for ever since she and Pandora had kept house they had longed for a real baby to be part of the household.

"What's in the other room?" demanded Jill, more interested in the house than in the baby for the moment.

Rory flung open the door into a real cottage parlour, with flowering plants on the window-sills, photographs of the family, including the "angels." There was a bookcase full of fairy-tales and folk-lore, two cushioned chairs, one on each side of the fireplace, which was filled with huge pine-cones all ready to light, and a round table in the middle of the room held Pandora's fretwork and Rory's paint-boxes, pencils, and books.

"Come and look in the cupboard," cried Rory, and she flung open the corner cupboard in the kitchen and proudly displayed a great many covered jam-pots.

"Pan and I make all our own jam and cakes, and sometimes we give tea-parties and bake hot scones in the oven, and we wash and iron the curtains, and clean the windows and scrub the floor. Father said if he gave us a house we must learn how to keep it, and Wendy always gives us yards of 'Hints to Young Housekeepers' for dictation, if she calls and finds things looking dirty."

"I wish *I* could scrub something," said Jill, looking

longingly into a cupboard near the door full of pails and brushes.

"Well, perhaps you shall some day; what a pity we've had the spring cleaning. I say, if the baby's going to live here, I'm afraid we must tell Pan; you see, she's got the other key, and she'll be so surprised to find it."

"Well, I don't mind; but, suppose she tells the other two?"

"No, she won't; and Cassandra and Pen won't find out, because now we've got a school with bells and things going all day there's no time."

"Well, tell her, then—it will be a good thing, because it will take such lots of pocket-money to bring up a baby."

"Let's get her a white frock."

"She'll want a name first. I say, let's call her Dilkusha —that's lovely and means ' Heart's Delight.' Now, you think of a second name."

"We always give classical names in this family—you know, things out of mythology—Father liked it."

"Well, think of one. I always get those mythological persons muddled up."

Rory suddenly jumped. "I know!"

"What?"

"Hyacinth—that's Greek, and we could call her Bluebell!"

"Super! I say, she doesn't like it; she's going to howl."

Dilkusha Hyacinth certainly set up such a roar that Rory was afraid the noise would be heard by Aunt Sally.

"She's hungry, the angel!" cried Jill.

"And we haven't got a bottle," wailed Rory.

"Yes, we have; there's the one Cassandra had for the pet lamb in the dairy; you wait here and I'll go and fill it with milk."

She was gone in an instant, and returned before Dilkusha Hyacinth had howled herself into a fit.

"There, my precious!" and Rory sat on a little wooden chair and rocked and hugged the baby violently, while Jill tipped the pet lamb's bottle perilously far down her throat.

But she was an obliging baby, and though she choked over it, she swallowed it too and then went off to sleep in Rory's enraptured arms.

"I am so hungry," sighed Jill.

"Well, there are lots of coconut biscuits in the cupboard; let's have some," said Rory; but before they could enjoy many of these luxuries she cried, "I say, it's nearly half-past six! We'll have to leave this precious —she's fast asleep—and go into the garden with the others, or that Laurette or Aunt Sally will ask us where we've been and worm out all our secrets."

The baby was laid on a cushioned chair and tied securely, the door was locked, and the two girls fled towards the kitchen garden.

But they hadn't gone far before they heard, "Hi, there!" and stood still.

Miss Billock, crossing the orchard grass, called loudly, "Come here, you two—Rory and Lucy, ain't it?"

"I'm *not* Lucy," said Jill indignantly; "the horridest name there is!"

"Well, you look like the Lucy girl who pulled up the parsley instead of the weeds yesterday," said Aunt Sally. "But, never mind, I don't care who you are; what I want is six strong young women to plant out some rows of lettuces."

"But I'm *not* strong!" exclaimed Jill in despair, for planting out lettuces seemed a tame ending to her exciting morning. "I'm very delicate; in fact, Mary Ellen was afraid I was in for a decline last night!"

"Well, there's nothing like fresh air and occupation for a person in a decline," said Aunt Sally cheerfully; "it's the new cure. In the old silly days when a gel was in a decline she sat in a stuffy room and did rows and rows of samplers till she died; now we take 'em out in the fresh air and let 'em plant rows and rows of lettuces and they get better in a jiffy. Come on; don't hump your shoulders like a camel, Lucy, or I'll ask that Rew girl to give you a few flower-pots to carry on your head."

Without listening to further protests, she stalked on her way, and soon pounced upon Pandora, Pauline, and two more strong young women busily trying to dodge her, and set them to their task on the lettuce bed.

"Where have you been?" demanded Pandora of Rory, feeling decidedly jealous that she should have been on an expedition of her own with the fascinating new girl.

"I don't see why I shouldn't go out with Jill if she wants me," answered Rory chillily, for Pandora had hinted the night before that Jill would not be likely to chum up with a kid of ten.

"I suppose you simply held on to her. What a little donkey you are; she'll only snub you."

"Will she? then let me tell you she *won't*. She thinks all that talk about kids is insane, and she and I have got the most thrilling secret you ever knew. So you can go on enjoying yourself with that hateful Pauline and that showing-off Julie, and leave me and Jill alone."

"Well, you needn't begin to be a spitfire as usual; you know I'd rather be with you—these girls are idiots. At least, Julie's all right, but we *must* make them enjoy themselves or they'll leave, and then where will Wendy be, and Idle Pines, and the angels and the Sanctuary?"

Mollified by Pandora's confession that she would rather be with her, and that the girls were idiots, Rory said sweetly, "Pan, *promise* you won't take the others if I tell you what's in the Sanctuary."

"The Sanctuary!—of course I won't. What is it?—do be quick. Don't tell me you have let that Jill catch a baby squirrel?"

"No, it isn't a baby squirrel."

"Well, what is it?"

"It's a *real* baby, and it's *ours*!"

CHAPTER 7

THE YOUNGEST GIRL IN THE SCHOOL

WHILE Jill thrilled a row of amateur gardeners with tales of her school life of the past, and Aunt Sally marched up and down like a general issuing orders and calling every one by wrong names, Rory poured into Pandora's astonished ears the tale of the Bluebell Baby.

"Do you mean to say you've stolen a baby and left it by itself in the Sanctuary?" gasped Pan.

"Stolen it!—don't be silly. It just appeared wrapped in a green shawl, and there was not any one in sight for miles. We had to put it somewhere, and the Sanctuary was the only place now the house is full of girls poking their noses everywhere."

"Pretty cool of you, I must say, to take Jill to the Sanctuary without a word to me."

"Well, I told her we'd have to tell you about the baby and she said she didn't mind."

"How condescending of her! And what are you going to do *next*?"

"Directly after breakfast and prayers, we must fly there and feed her before lessons."

"A lot of time there will be to bring up babies before lessons—with beds to make, rooms to tidy, and the ponies to look after!"

"Well, we must fly round, and Pen and Cassandra will do the ponies for once."

"If you've taken Jill to the Sanctuary, I don't see why I shouldn't bring Julie."

"She'll spoil everything," wailed Rory, thinking that if two more foster-mothers were to be given to Dilkusha

Bluebell the less often it would be her turn to nurse her.

"No, she won't; she's awfully nice, and doesn't belong to the 'ordinaries,' like Pauline and Nancy."

When Cassandra was a tiny girl she always described people who did not interest her as "ordinaries," and ever since the name had been used by the family when they wanted to be scathing.

"Then I'll have to ask Jill about the baby," cried Rory, and she started off to her fellow-conspirator and whispered her tale of woe.

"Is Julie the one with the long plait and freckles on her nose?"

"Yes; a showing-off person, I call her."

"She looks rather decent, I think; let's have her."

So the tale was passed along the lettuce rows to Julie, who swore secrecy, and also to fly about her tasks after breakfast, so that a visit could be paid to the refugee in the Sanctuary.

When their tasks were accomplished there were exactly fifteen minutes left before morning school, and the four girls had to scamper to the pine-wood.

Bluebell was fast asleep, and the sight of her chubby loveliness amidst the folds of the green shawl made Pandora and Julie eager to adopt her on the spot.

"All the same it's idiotic; we can't keep a secret baby," remonstrated Julie. "We ought to tell the police."

"The police!" cried Jill and Rory together, casting eyes of scorn at the hard-hearted Julie, and Jill added, "If we do, she'll be hauled off to some orphan asylum."

"Our policeman wouldn't," remarked Pan; "he'd go to bed and say he was off duty if we took a baby to him; he's only interested in people who don't light their bicycle lamps."

"It will be lonely for her here; I can't think what we shall do with her at night," said Jill, looking worried; "but surely a sanctuary in a wood with four people to love her and lots of bottles is better than an asylum full of other babies smelling of yellow soap and flannel."

"I *do* wish she'd wake," said Rory.

"It's nearly nine o'clock; we'll have to go," announced Pandora. "Perhaps she'll go on sleeping; the lamb's bottle holds heaps, you know."

"We'll ask Wendy if we can come to the wood at eleven," cried Rory, and the baby was covered up cosily and Julie torn from the beauties of the Sanctuary kitchen, and they all rushed to the school-room.

Fortunately for the baby, it was possible to carry out Rory's suggestion that they should return to the wood at eleven, as Miss Wendell had very broad ideas about the morning recreation.

The girls worked hard for two hours, and were then entirely free for fifty minutes. If they wished to play organised games, Dorothy, Miss Bruce, and often Wendy herself, were ready to play, too, but if they preferred to scramble about the woods, garden, do carpentry, or even go for a run to the sea or village, they were allowed to do so, for she believed they came back all the fresher to their school work if time were given them to enjoy their own particular resources; and the only rule she made was that they must do *something*—not loll about chattering or reading, and they were also expected to tell some person in authority where they were going.

No sooner was school dismissed than the four girls sought out Wendy, and Pandora made the request, "Please may we all go into the pine-wood? We don't want to play tennis, nor practise archery, a bit."

"And what will you do in the pine-wood?"

"We'll be busy in the Sanctuary."

Wendy smiled.

"Very well, then; but don't forget, no eating between meals. There are rather too many jam-pots in the Sanctuary."

Such howls issued from the Sanctuary that the four foster-mothers rushed headlong to the rescue, and found poor Bluebell a most indignant and hungry baby, screaming with wrath and discomfort, for her cords were decidedly tight.

"She wants food first; have you washed the bottle and filled it, Rory?"—Rory rushed to her nursemaid's duties. "Then she must be bathed; babies——"

"I'll bath her," cried Pan; "I'm so used to washing the dogs."

"Dilkusha is *not* a dog," said Jill more coldly still; "and the spine of an infant——"

"I don't see why *you* should have her all the time," objected Julie.

"I haven't got her all the time—there, precious, the nasty cords are undone. There's Mummy Rory with the *loveliest* bottle; and if you like we'll draw lots for the bath."

"*Do* let me hold her while she drinks it," said Rory plaintively, for she knew there was little chance for *her* to bathe an infant's spine.

"Very well"—Jill gave up Bluebell—"where on earth shall we get hot water? We can't put her in cold and have her down with pneumonia."

"That's easy enough," cried Pandora, and she put a light to the logs in the kitchen range and set the kettle over to boil, while Julie, determined that favours should be equally divided, cut three oblong pieces of paper.

"Rory can't bath her, so she needn't draw," she remarked.

"Oh, of *course* not!" cried Rory; "I know as much about babies as *you* do, anyhow."

"Of course you do," said Jill soothingly; "but we simply *can't* spare you to bath; you're so awfully good about washing the bottle, and if she gets a sour bottle she'll die—so it's *most* important."

Comforted, Rory hugged and jogged Bluebell up and down violently, while Julie tipped the lamb's bottle down her mouth, anxious that she should receive the much needed nourishment quickly.

"There! she's had every drop!" she cried, as the baby gave a final choke.

"And the water is ready," announced Pan.

There was no bath, and the washing-up pan was pronounced to be too small for a baby of Bluebell's plumpness, so Jill routed out a deep tin pail, lots were drawn, and it fell to Jill.

"I wonder if it's too hot?" said Jill, feeling the water in the pail with the tip of her finger.

"You try it with your elbow," said Julie. "Our old Nannie always did—if it doesn't go red you can put in any kid without boiling it."

Jill obediently dipped her dimpled elbow in the pail, and as it did not redden immediately, she lifted the kicking Bluebell into it tenderly.

Such a yell came from the unfortunate baby that Pandora rushed to stuff the windows with newspapers.

"There, I've scalded her—thanks to *your* advice," said Jill bitterly, grasping the slippery baby so nervously that she slid like an eel back into the pail and yelled more loudly than ever.

"You're torturing her!" wailed Rory, wringing her hands in despair.

"You must have a froggy elbow," explained Julie. "Pour some more water in, Pandora; she isn't really scalded."

Pandora generously emptied a can of cold water into the pail, and Bluebell's next plunge made her wail in despair.

"That's enough," advised Pandora, when Jill had soused Bluebell from top to toe, and was then squeezing spongefuls of water down her back, murmuring words of comfort as she did so.

"I *must* get all the soap off her. At that school I went to—the indigestion one—they made us fill the bath up twice with cold water after a bath, so that we shouldn't leave any soap on our skin. Give me another tea-cloth, Rory; this one is soaking."

But not only Bluebell and the tea-cloths were soaking: Jill was, too, before the ablutions were finished.

"I say, she ought to have some breathing exercises after this; she looks awfully blue," said Julie.

Jill gave Bluebell a final rub and commanded Rory to pass her the parcel.

The mysterious parcel brought by Jill was opened and a white nightgown, finely tucked, and beautifully embroidered, and a white petticoat were taken out of it.

"What are you going to do with those things?"

"Dress her in them, until we've made her proper clothes. We can tie up the sleeves and loop her up at the waist with a sash."

The garments were put over Bluebell's protesting head, while Rory, Pan, and Julie strove to make her forget her woes by dangling every object in the Sanctuary before her bewildered eyes and capering like dancing dervishes. When Rory made cymbals of two bright saucepan lids and clashed them together noisily, she was so charmed that she smiled, which, Jill said, proved she was musical.

"I think she's rather too big to be a long-tailed baby," criticised Pan.

"And I think it's about time I had something to do with her, if I'm going to have such an expensive hobby as a baby this term," broke in Julie.

"You both take her out in the wood while Rory and I clear up all this mess," said Jill generously, for now that her maternal duties were over she was longing to mop up the floor.

"You had better get another bottle ready, too," suggested Pan. "There isn't much more time, and she'll have to be fed and put to sleep before we leave her. I say, she's beginning to howl again."

The unfortunate baby, suffering from a too hasty meal, during which she had been jogged up and down so furiously it had woefully disagreed with her, followed by a scalding bath, and then an ice-cold one before she could get her breath, as well as other well-meant cruelties, certainly *did* howl; but a handful of orange pine-cones tossed in the air by Pandora, and the sudden dart of a squirrel, made her forget her injuries for a moment, and she smiled so adorably through her tears that Julie and Pandora were as much enraptured with her as the others. Fortunately for her little insides, she fell asleep over Pandora's shoulder before Rory appeared with the lamb's bottle once more well filled.

She was tucked up in the chair again, and her four foster-mothers returned to Wendy's English literature lesson in such attentive moods that she congratulated herself on a rule which left her pupils time to develop their own innocent resources!

After luncheon things were more difficult, because to make up for the early hour of rising the girls were made to rest flat on their backs in the open air, and could either read, talk, or meditate until the bell rang for afternoon lessons.

"My decline is so bad this afternoon," remarked Jill, collapsing on a rug under the big cedar-tree, "I shouldn't mind lying in this delicious shade for half an hour and making up another chapter of ' Lost and Found,' while somebody else brings up that blessed kid."

"What on earth is ' Lost and Found '?" inquired Pandora.

"It's a remarkable romance I have been making up ever since I was two; I tell it to myself every night, and at the ordinary school I used to tell it to the girls in my dormitory too. There was one kid so thrilled by it that she made her mother—a frightfully swanky person who was a countess—ask me to stay with them so that she would hear some more in the holidays, but Moti wouldn't let me go."

"*Do* tell us some," entreated Rory.

"Perhaps I will some day, but you'll howl. I do myself sometimes, it's so awfully tragic. I say, what about Dilkusha?"

"Pan and I will go," offered Julie. "We can't all disappear—Pauline is getting suspicious, and here she is. She simply hangs on to us."

With Miss Bruce conscientiously reading to what Rory called "a crowd of ordinaries" on the veranda, and the elder girls all too comfortable to bother about tiresome juniors, it was fairly easy for Pan and Julie to slip away to the pine wood, and feed Bluebell and rock her into a doze again.

"It's the night I'm worrying about," groused Jill to Pandora and Julie during the afternoon."

"We'll ask Jessie Mills to take her," said Pandora suddenly.

"Who is Jessie Mills?" demanded Jill.

"A girl without a mother who lives in a cottage close to the wood. She's only fifteen, but she keeps house and has brought up about a dozen baby brothers and sisters. She'll smuggle Bluebell somewhere and won't tell, because she's a secret friend of Rory's and mine."

While Julie and Jill fed and amused Bluebell, Rory and Pan flew to fetch Jessie, who seemed slightly dazed when told she was expected to minister to a lost baby, and very much harassed by the thought of those she had left in her own home.

"Mind, it's a secret, Jessie; we don't want the poor darling to go to the workhouse."

"Yes, Miss Pandora; I won't let on—not me; but you *did* ought to tell the perlice, and that's the truth."

"Then we just *won't*," broke in Jill; "don't be absurd, Jessie Mills, please. What we want is a nurse for this angel until we can find a home where we can all go to visit her—we'll pay, of course—for we can't keep her here all day."

"She's got a belly-ache already, Miss," said Jessie wisely.

"What on earth do you mean?" cried Jill indignantly.

"It's her milk turned a bit, Miss; you didn't ought to jog her like that while she takes her bottle. Our Tommy, he's a rare one for the belly-ache and I always lays him down after his food—like this, Miss——" and the motherly Jessie put Bluebell across her lap and patted her soothingly.

Forced to confess that Jessie understood babies, Jill said, "Well, will you take care of her to-night?"

"I couldn't, Miss; you see, I've got three of 'em in the bed already. Mabel she'd yell for Father like a shot if she saw a strange babby, and he'd have the perlice in a jiffy. He wouldn't 'old with stealing babies, wouldn't Father!"

"She *isn't* stolen! How tiresome you are, Jessie," cried Rory.

"And why, for goodness' sake, can't you put Mabel into somebody else's bed?" asked Pandora.

"I couldn't, Miss; Father's got all the boys, and if I put Mabel in the chair-bed along with Billy and Maudie they'd get telling her there's tigers in the pigsties and she'd roar the 'ouse down."

"What a horrid person Mabel is!" exclaimed Rory, and Julie said severely: "I don't think you are bringing her up at all well, Jessie; but the question is, what shall we do with this angel?"

"If you got a bed for her, Miss, I'd slip across two or three times this evening, and again when Father goes to work at half-past five. She won't take no 'arm then if she's warm and her food don't turn in her."

"We can get the old cradle out of the attic," suggested Pandora.

"And a blanket from each of our beds," cried Julie; "jolly lucky for Bluebell she's got two Spartan mothers!"

So Jessie's offer was accepted, and the old wooden cradle from the attic was conveyed after many hair-breadth escapes to the Sanctuary, and Bluebell, still suffering from what the plain-spoken Jessie called "belly-ache," and decidedly cross, was left to the care of her new nurse.

But that night, when the other inmates of Somnus were soundly sleeping, Jill lay awake, tormented by a conscience.

Suppose Jessie forgot.

Suppose a fox climbed into the window and carried her off as a dainty morsel for his cubs!

Suppose some wandering gipsy heard her cry and stole her for the sake of the hand-made Belgian lace on her nightgown?

She sat up in bed. There wasn't a sound in the house and the moon was playing hide-and-seek behind dark clouds. It was terrible to think of Bluebell all alone in the wood.

"I simply can't stand it another moment," murmured Jill, and, creeping out of bed, she drew on her dressing-gown and slippers and slipped downstairs to the side door she and Rory had unlocked that morning.

Then she made her way to the wood. No sooner had she reached the gorse-bushes, which loomed out of the shadows before the Sanctuary like tall sentinels, than she almost screamed with fright. Two windows in the Sanctuary were lit up—the gipsy must have arrived!

Trembling, she peeped into the window and gave a gasp of surprise. On the kitchen table stood a lighted lantern, and on the stoutest chair sat Aunt Sally, making strange, clucking sounds at Bluebell, who certainly seemed to be suffering more than ever from the disease about which Jessie knew so much.

Suddenly Aunt Sally caught up the baby, just as though she were a roll of garden-netting, wrapped her in a blanket, seized the lantern and left the house, giving Jill only just time to whisk behind the pine-trees.

She marched like a grenadier to her own cottage and shut the door firmly, and Jill was left to return miserably to her bed.

"*Now* there'll be a row," she remarked, hugging her cold toes. "Well, I've gone and done it again, and I suppose Miss Wendell will never believe I was trying to be really good and useful; I simply must leave off putting my fingers into other people's sickening pies," and after this resolution she sank into a restless sleep.

The next morning she was heavy-eyed and inclined to be gloomy.

"What about Bluebell?" whispered Pandora. "Oughtn't one of us to slip to the Sanctuary?"

"There isn't any Bluebell," said Jill.

"*What!*" The three foster-mothers stood open-mouthed.

"No; Aunt Sally kidnapped her late last night. I expect she's planted her out in a box by this time and given her a Latin name as well as a Greek one—poor little kid! There'll be a row; but I did it, so *you* needn't worry."

Before Jill had finished speaking the four were summoned to Wendy's room.

The head mistress was calm, and did not betray by word or look what she thought of their latest escapade; she simply said,—"Well, Pandora and Julie, this is your fourth day at school, and the second time I have had to send for you both. I fear it looks as though you were not intended for a school where Liberty reigns, and you would both be better where rules and mistresses are strict and your every action supervised; in fact, I think it would be just as well to ask Miss Bruce if she will kindly act as watch-dog to the girls I can't trust to use their freedom rightly. I am sorry to see that Marguerite and Aurora seem to be following your example already. Now, Pandora, I want an explanation, please."

"But it's *our* baby," broke in Jill; "at least I'm its mother and Rory is its mummy—Pandora and Julie are just going to help pay for her education and all that——"

"Please speak intelligently, Marguerite, and tell me exactly where that poor little atom came from."

With many interruptions from Rory, Jill told the tale, adding loyally that Pandora, Julie, and Jessie had strongly advised telling a policeman.

"But why not tell *me*?" cried Wendy, "or Madame or Miss Dillon? Surely you had enough intelligence to know that somebody is sure to be desperately anxious about a lost child."

"Oh, Wendy!" cried Rory; "it wasn't lost; it was put there, and don't pretend you don't believe it. And we didn't tell any one because Jill says Orphan Asylums are beastly places."

"And I've always wanted a child of my own," added Jill. "I've got such good ideas about——"

"Killing them!" suggested Wendy. "I am particularly anxious that the girls of Idle Pines shall be distinguished for their capability and intelligence in cases of emergency; but I fear I shall have to wait a long time for that if Julie's porridge and Marguerite's ideas on infant welfare are an example of your domestic education. When Miss Billock traced the screams she heard to that poor baby last night it was suffering from the ignorance of four girls who were quite old enough to know better. Now please tell me what you intended to do with the poor little thing?"

Jill explained volubly.

"Oh, Wendy, I *do* wish you wouldn't look like the Snow Queen or somebody *icy* like that," wailed Rory.

"What are you going to do with the precious?"

"Find her mother, of course."

"But you *can't,* unless you're a seventh child of a seventh child born on a Sunday——"

Wendy sent for the village policeman at once, who took a great many notes with a stumpy pencil in a note-book and asked Jill and Rory so many questions, that the latter had no hope at all of not being marched off to the Tower of London before nightfall for kidnapping a baby.

But though handbills were put everywhere and careful inquiries made in all directions for her lawful owners, nobody claimed Bluebell, who, cured of her sufferings, was installed in the old nursery, cooing like a turtle-dove.

"Don't come telling me she's one of *Them*, Miss Rory," cried Mary Ellen, "with legs on her like that more likely she's been brought up on Benger's than fairy food. Not that I say *They* hadn't a hand in the finding of her, with her lying by the white christening-bell and all. You and Miss Jill were fairy-led, I'll be bound."

After a week's vain search Wendy summoned the whole school and asked each girl to write on a slip of paper what she advised about the fate of Bluebell.

Pauline, who resented not being taken into the secret at first, and was not exactly keen on babies or spending her pocket-money on them, wrote that she thought it right to advertise in *The Times* at once for a rich person to adopt her. Meg Connell suggested that Madame Clément—chosen because her absence would also mean the absence of a French lesson—should journey to London and drop the baby into a basket provided by some

Foundling Hospital; but with one accord all the other girls gave the same advice: "Adopt her, and we'll pay."

"Very well; we will," said Wendy, smiling. "She will be for the use of the school; instead of buying a big doll or borrowing a village baby. For after her sufferings in the Sanctuary, I feel sure you will all be the better for some lessons in mothercraft. But remember, if you do adopt her, you must attend to her yourselves—dress her, make her clothes, bath her, take her out and amuse her—except at night, when Mary Ellen will attend to her. Are you all willing?"

"Rather!" cried everybody except Pauline, who murmured that she should strike if "taking care of kids were added to taking care of Aunt Sally's seedlings!" but nobody cared for Pauline's opinion, and Laurette fetched Bluebell and she was solemnly adopted by the whole school.

"Well, even if Wendy did take away our liberty for a week, Jill and I had a *real* adventure—not a silly porridge-making thing," said Rory triumphantly to Pandora.

"Well, you needn't think you're the school heroine," answered Pandora scathingly.

"I don't"—Rory was still triumphant—"but anyhow, you can't say any longer that I'm the-youngest-girl-in-the-school!"

CHAPTER 8

"THE ISLE OF CIRCE"

Miss Wendell was no believer in despotic government for kings nor for schools, so when Laurette presented her with the names of those who objected to Rule IV, she called the girls together and explained why she had made it.

"I see no reason why the village should be out of bounds," she said, "as long as you go there in twos or threes; but, unfortunately, there is a small shop there where quantity is studied more than quality. Once we had Pandora and Rory seriously ill through spending their pocket-money on a feast, which, fortunately for every one else, they were greedy enough to keep to themselves! I don't want any more invalids of that sort. But suppose some one makes a suggestion which leaves you the freedom of the village without temptation to eat rather deadly sweets."

"You could put the shop out of bounds," suggested Cassandra, who only liked sweets of the very best variety.

"No," said Laurette wisely, for she knew more about the ways of schoolgirls than Cassandra; "a sweet-shop out of bounds is too tempting for some people," and she glanced at Jill, who had already given her some bad moments.

"*Much* too tempting," said Jill piously; "though not to me, because I *never* eat disgusting sweets."

"But why can't we *promise* we won't buy them?" asked Rory.

"That would certainly be a good rule, Rory," said Wendy—"if you are all willing——"

"I know," cried Pandora, always ready with ideas; "let us give our word of honour we will only buy plain chocolate there once a week."

"But I don't like plain chocolate," wailed a voice.

"Then we could make toffee for the chocolate haters in the laundry on wet Saturday afternoons, couldn't we, Miss Wendell?" suggested Eve.

"Yes, as long as you don't burn too many saucepans, leave everything tidy, and only eat the toffee after luncheon," said Wendy. "But the penalty, should any one break their promise? I will leave that to you, too."

"I suggest that the penalty for buying disgusting sweets is a good dose of Turkey rhubarb—that's worse than castor-oil," said Jill, who knew she ran no risk of suffering the penalty herself.

And as everybody agreed that the punishment fitted the crime, the matter was settled and Rule IV abolished.

The next thing to be done was the election of four leaders or under-prefects, a rather difficult task for Penelope and Laurette, because nobody to whom they offered the honour seemed very keen on having it.

"Awfully kind of you, but *no thanks*," said Eve. "I'm rather keen on looking after young chickens and young cabbages, but I don't see why I should be always tearing after those wretched kids; I pretend I'm asleep when they rampage in the dormitory now."

Isobel Clifton, who was not "bossy" after all, but quiet and shy, and anxious not to be noticed, was distressed at the idea of having to play mentor and begged to be excused. "I'm such a awful coward," she pleaded, "and I should never *dare* to give advice to girls like Julie and Jill."

Mary Leslie accepted, though she warned the prefects that she was not going to make herself old and ugly before her time with worrying about a lot of juniors. "I'll snub them well, especially that Pauline kid and that little horror with the awful name—Gladys Shaw, but I won't preach and make myself hated, so now you know."

"There, Cassandra, *you'll* have to be a leader," cried the worried Penelope.

"*What!* I suppose you'll make me put on a leather belt and an awful hat with a strap under my chin next! Don't be absurd, Penelope. You know very well that Pan and Rory never take the least notice of anything I suggest. Besides, I never have a second to myself now Idle Pines is turned into a bear-garden, and I certainly shan't spend the little time I have in being a school-marm."

Miss Wendell was appealed to privately, and she invited the four girls to tea in the library, but was wise enough not to mention juniors nor leaders until just before they left. Then she said casually, "By the way, I hear Penelope and Laurette have asked you to help them with the younger girls. It was foolish of them, as you are all quite unfitted for leadership. I should have chosen Marguerite Beville for one myself, though she is young."

"Unfitted for leadership! Chosen that chit of a Jill!" In a moment the four girls were burning with a desire to be prefects.

"Oh, I say Miss Wendell, that's pretty stiff!" cried Eve. "I think I could look after a few juniors better than that little minx."

"Not at all. Jill has ambition, and any amount of energy, two things necessary for leadership. She has ideals, too, and that is what we need in the school, and I hear *you* say you can't be bothered to take responsibilities."

This was terrible, for Miss Wendell plainly meant they were shirkers, and Cassandra was cut to the heart that Wendy should think Jill had higher ideals than herself.

"But Wendy," she remonstrated, "it's such a thankless

task always acting the school-marm to a crowd of schoolgirls who criticise everything you do or say."

"Then don't be a school-marm—it's the very thing I wish to avoid—and make an effort to do and say the right thing and you won't be criticised."

"As a matter of fact I *was* thinking of taking it on," said Eve, and Cassandra said hastily, "And *I* will if you really want me to, Wendy."

"I said I would," explained Mary, "though I must confess I said, too, that I didn't want to be bothered."

Isobel murmured, "I'll *try*, but I'm not a bit good at preaching."

"But, my dear girls, I don't *want* you to preach! I simply want you to help me to carry out an idea—to let you rule *yourselves*, for that is the way, I feel sure, to banish most of the grievances we find in every school, as well as helping you in after life to stand alone and work out your own salvation. I may be wrong, and we are sure to have some failures and many difficulties—the greatest at present is that ours is such a new school, no pupil as yet feels enthusiastic enough to work for its future honour. But before the year is over, if we all throw ourselves heart and soul into the building up of my idea, I believe we shall be proud of a school that has a reputation for training girls to look after themselves as well as others, and capable of doing useful work as well as ornamental—girls who do not collapse directly school bells and school rules no longer call them to their duty."

"But what can *we* do?"

"Set a good example, of course, by being self-reliant, generous, kind, courageous and well-mannered without being priggish, and not interfering with things that don't matter in the least. I will tell you a secret. I don't blame Jill and Rory for getting up at dawn to propitiate the fairies, even though it did throw an orphan on my hands! They will never forget that early morning in the Glen, and perhaps many years hence the memory of it will light up some dark and dreary day."

"But it's such a bore to be a saint all the time," groaned Eve.

"It would bore me terribly to have a school for saints," said Wendy, smiling; "but it would delight me to see all of you helping me to found a school of Happiness, and you *can* help me by interesting the younger girls."

The result of Wendy's lecture was that the four girls went to Penelope and Laurette, and Eve as spokeswoman remarked casually, "I say, girls, we've been thinking it over and we'll back you up with those kids."

"And so you ought," said Laurette ungratefully.

"But if we do," cautioned Cassandra, "remember we want to do the thing properly—I mean, have some plan of action."

Astounded at this from the gloomy girl-hating Cassandra, Pen woke up and became really interested.

"We ought to adopt Scout law," said Mary, who was always ready to quote other people's ideas, having few of her own, "and each make ourselves responsible, you know, for so many girls."

"Patrols," said Eve. "There are twenty-eight girls—we could each have seven."

"I bar that Pauline kid and Gladys Shaw," broke in Mary.

"I shan't have Pan and Rory," cried Cassandra. "You know what that means, Pen; if I make a simple suggestion they say, 'Don't boss,' or 'You're not Wendy,' or something like that."

"Better draw lots," suggested Laurette.

"Oh, please, don't," wailed Isobel; "if we do, I'm sure to get Jill or Julie, and I could never tackle either of them."

But the others agreed that to draw lots was the fairest

way, and, strangely enough, both Jill and Julie, as well as Rory, were among Cassandra's seven.

Pandora and Pauline fell to Eve, and the objectionable Gladys Shaw became a burden on Isobel's anxious shoulders.

Wendy had always maintained that whatever were the faults of her four pupils half-heartedness was not one of them, and Cassandra proved she was right by throwing herself heart and soul into the task of improving the ideals of her special seven. Stifling her dislike for "silly schoolgirls," she tried to look amiable, and, adopting an elder sisterly manner, she invited her protégées to the round summer-house on the cliff, and plunged into Greek heroes at once, though Rory spoilt everything by fidgeting, and saying, "I don't see why we should all sit here in a row, listening to tales we have known ever since we were born, while everybody else is playing cricket."

"I say, oughtn't we to go?" asked Julie, frightfully bored with Greek heroes. "It's our turn to lay supper, Jill, and I want to get some flowers from the meadow."

"There's lots of time," said Cassandra, frowning. "I've been thinking how awfully nice it would be if we got up a Greek play as a surprise for Miss Wendell."

"Would there be anything to learn?" asked Rory guardedly, and Julie cried, "But why a *Greek* play? They're so dull. Once at Hill House we got up a pierrot troupe and wore black dresses with scarlet pom-poms, and gave an entertainment to help the cricket club. I know lots of comic songs, and even Miss Abbott said it was jolly good."

"Pierrots! Comic songs!" cried the outraged and scholarly Cassandra; "I mean a play worth doing and worth acting and worth remembering. Any brainless idiot can be a *Pierrot*."

"Then let's pretend we are brainless idiots," suggested

Rory, who felt attracted by a black dress with scarlet pom-poms.

"Shouldn't we dress up if we were Greeks?" said Jill soothingly, for she felt sorry for Cassandra, who for some unknown reason seemed terribly keen on improving their minds.

"Of course we should," promised Cassandra; "something *very* simple, you know, just short tunics and sandals and bare arms and legs."

"With lots of midge-cream on them," said Jill. "Midges must *love* Greeks," and she rubbed her ankles wretchedly. "What play could we have?"

"I don't know; we must think about it. Let's all meet here before supper on Friday and decide."

So it was settled, though Julie remarked that she didn't think much of a surprise that would bore the whole school to death.

"If you have to lay supper you had better be quick," cried Cassandra. "Now, remember, don't say a word to any one."

Cassandra retired to rack her brains about a Greek play, the others ran to the cricket-field, and Julie and Jill to their duties at the supper-table.

"There!" cried Jill, setting down a china bowl of cuckoo flowers massed with golden marsh marigolds; "doesn't that look ripping? Don't move the lettuce, those crinkly green leaves look lovely by the mauvy flowers. Wasn't Pauline's table *awful* last night with the beetroot salad bang up against a jar of bluebells? I nearly fainted. That's the worst of having an artistic temperament."

"Aunt Sally says we can grow what we like for the flower show in July," said Julie; "bags me sweet peas."

"And I'll have Canterbury bells—lots of blue and white ones, they're such topping things; and one never knows if one of *Them* isn't tucked up in one of the bells," said

Jill. "I say, I do wish Cassandra weren't so learned, don't you?"

"Even Greeks can have fun," said Julie, a remark which made Jill begin to form outrageous plans immediately.

A rather bored-looking party arrived in the summer-house the following Friday, and Cassandra's heart sank, for she was naturally despondent, and she felt she would never transform these tiresome girls into enthusiastic idealists.

"Have you thought of something stunning?" demanded Julie.

"And tragic," said Jill. "We'd better wail—Greek choruses always do and it's frightfully impressive."

"I've been thinking it over," said Cassandra; "and if we want to get up something quickly it must be simple for a beginning; we'll do something bigger later. Let us have Greek statuary in the woods. There won't be a thing to learn, and we'll only have to get the dresses and practise the posing."

"Statues," cried Julie; "then I'm out of it! I suffer too severely from that awful disease called ' The Giggles ' to be a statue."

"Besides, statues don't wear any clothes," said Meg primly.

"And I don't want to be Aurora," objected Rory, seeing this part in Cassandra's eye. "I've worn that old dress such lots of times I'm sick of it."

"I think it sounds jolly," cried Jill, and the "ordinaries," Mavis, Winifred, and Diana, at once agreed with her.

"Tell us what you propose, Cassandra."

"I thought we would make a little setting for the most well-known Grecian deities in the gardens and woods. Wendy always gives a mythology lesson on Thursday afternoons; without telling her the secret, we could invite every one to see the 'divinities' that day. I shan't be a statue, just a Greek maiden gliding before them chanting a few lines in blank verse about each one."

"I'd rather be a Greek maiden gliding about than a statue," remarked Rory.

"Very well, you *can*," said Cassandra, forgetting to be tactful. "But remember, you'll have to learn your part, and if you make a muddle of it and spoil everything, you can go and be a Pierrot for all I care! "

"I'd rather be a statue than learn blank verse; it's so jolly hard," said Jill, and Rory hastily announced that she had no time for a Greek maiden's duties.

"I can't remember a single 'divinity' except Venus," remarked Mavis; "and it seems so conceited to pose as a beautiful person of that sort."

"I'll be Pan," announced Jill with determination. "I don't care if he *is* a boy. I simply love him, and I'm like him, too, because I adore wandering over mountains and rocks and woods and having people dance round me and teasing them. Besides, Pan wears a goatskin, and that will keep off the midges—a jolly good thing for a statue who doesn't want to yell while Cassandra spouts blank verse."

"Sometimes Pan is represented as half-goat and half-man, and sometimes as a youth wearing a chlamys—a sort of light cloak," said Cassandra, seizing the opportunity to instruct her charges in Greek customs; "but you can wear a goat-skin if you like; there's that one in the attic with the moths in it, Rory."

"But I'd rather be bitten by midges than eaten by moths," cried Jill, and Meg wailed, "What shall I be? Do tell us some, Cassandra—Jill and Julie won't let any one speak."

Cassandra obediently "told some," and Winifred instantly chose to be Mercury; Mavis, Pomona; and

Meg, Iris. Diana was, of course, Diana, and Rory was persuaded to be Aurora by Jill, who vowed she was the nicest divinity after Pan.

"Let's have Bluebell as Cupid," cried Jill; "she'd look such a cherub, with nothing on at all except a little quiver of arrows."

But Cassandra was indignant at the flippancy of the suggestion, though Rory remarked she thought it a splendid idea, and Bluebell could be a "wound-up" statue, so it wouldn't matter if she kicked and gurgled.

"This isn't a ' Mrs. Jarley's Waxwork Show,'" said Cassandra coldly. "Do be serious, please. Julie, you haven't chosen."

"I'll be that beautiful sorceress—you know, the one who lived on an island and turned Ulysses' sailors into pigs and things."

"Do you mean Circe?" asked Cassandra.

"Yes, that's the one; I'd love to be a sorceress."

"Very well; it *will* be rather effective," said Cassandra rather absently, for she wanted the blank verse to be original, and was dying to get away to compose it.

"The abode of Circe was guarded by lions and wolves," quoted Rory. "I *do* wish I'd thought of her; we could get the lion skin off the hall floor and stuff it with sawdust."

"We must choose the places, practise posing, and see about the dresses at once," said Cassandra. "All be here to-morrow at the same time and we'll have a rehearsal."

During the next few weeks all Cassandra's protégées —except Rory—learnt more about Greek mythology than several learned school mistresses had been able to impart to them for years.

"She's awfully clever," objected Julie, "but she bosses it so. Why can't *we* have some ideas too?"

"I've got lots," remarked Jill. "Listen to this realistic suggestion: it will bring down the house—I mean the wood"—and in a solemn whisper she informed Julie of a plan which made that mischief-loving person hug herself with joy.

"Shall we tell Rory?" she asked.

"No, she'll get into such a row with Cassandra, and they spar quite enough already."

As for Cassandra, she was forced to ask for "Sanctuary" several times while she wrestled with blank verse, and also absently ate a little of the jam store.

The dresses of the divinities were so simple they caused little anxiety, and Jill's clever fingers were very useful in making a silver-winged hat for Mercury and golden wings for Iris, as well as silver-paper covered sandals.

When everything was accomplished, Miss Wendell was presented with a very classical-looking scroll on which was written the request that she would bring her pupils to wander beneath the shadows of Mount Olympus the following Thursday at the hour of three.

Consumed with curiosity, and delighted at the idea of the novelty of having a mythology lesson in the woods, the junior girls especially awaited Thursday afternoon with impatience.

At three o'clock exactly, Cassandra, clad in flowing Greek garments, her pretty hair caught in a Greek knot and held by a green fillet, her bare feet thrust into sandals, and carrying a scroll, appeared to glide before the party to Olympus, and she certainly looked more classical than her followers, for Wendy had made herself comfortable in her oldest garden-hat—hidden by Pen and just rediscovered.

Madame Clément wore very high-heeled shoes and carried an embroidered bag containing a fan and various remedies for midge-bites; and Aunt Sally in her flannel blouse and tweed skirt, and the famous little hat perched on her forehead, looked more as if she were *en route* for the potato-field than Olympus.

Miss Dillon was in a severely cut coat and skirt, Miss Bruce in a frilly muslin frock, and Dorothy carried a flaring scarlet sunshade.

Cassandra led the way to the orchard first, where in the dappled sunlight under the apple-trees stood the lovely statue of Pomona, the goddess of orchard and fruit-trees. Mavis, on a stone pedestal, posed with every limb immovable, her bare arms held out, and laden with blossoming branches, with the tiny fruit just forming.

Cassandra unrolled her scroll and related some of the virtues of the lovely Pomona in blank verse, which astonished Wendy, while the juniors, apparently innocent and admiring, did everything on earth to make the goddess laugh—without result, for Mavis was a stolid " ordinary."

" *Très jolie*," cried Madame. " *Tiens!*—but she will suffer for this, *la pauvre enfant!* To-night, this goddess she will beg for a little ointment truly—the arms and the legs with nothing—*là! là!*"

Cassandra then sped towards the rose-garden, where Penelope's white doves cooed plaintively, and a big stone dolphin spurted silver water over a goldfish in a fountain, and everybody stood in a row and cried " Oh! *how* pretty," except Madame, who said, " Truly, this one is *superbe*! "

Standing on the dolphin's back, ready to speed on her way, was Winifred as Mercury, the messenger god, her hair hidden under a silver-winged cap, her long slender limbs draped lightly, one hand upraised, the other bearing the caduceus, or herald's staff.

There was very little blank verse about Mercury, because, in spite of constant practice, it was impossible for Winifred to balance herself so precariously for long, and Cassandra hurried the visitors away before disaster occurred.

Away went Cassandra, down the long path where purple and white lilacs nodded their scented heads over

rows of blue-eyed scillas and tall narcissi, to the dell
where Iris, the rainbow goddess, in her many-coloured
robes, and her golden wings outstretched, waited ready
to fly across the rainbow bridge which stretches between
earth and the heaven of the Immortals.

Meg was a pretty child, and as her coloured robes
were not scanty enough to be shocking, she was happy, and
and gazing up at the rainbow bridge of flowers which
swung in the trees above her, she really looked a charming
divinity.

"There! I wondered where all the purple anemones
had gone!" cried Aunt Sally almost before Cassandra
had "finished spouting."

Cassandra glided away quickly.

Not very far away in the wood they came upon Diana,
the huntress-goddess, in short robe, a quiver flying over
her shoulder and an arrow in her hand ready for the chase.

Cassandra was rather proud of the blank verse which
described Diana, and it was unfortunate that divinity
sneezed before it was over, except for the amusement it
gave to the juniors.

Cassandra hastened away to the Italian garden, which
lay on the west side of Idle Pines, where amidst the tall
cypress trees stood a bronze winged-horse. Behind it,
on the pedestal, holding reins of rose and gold-coloured
flowers was Aurora, the goddess of dawn, clad in a violet-
tinged mantle, a star on her forehead, a torch in her hand,
ready to drive her steed through the gates of heaven to
herald the coming of the great sun-god.

"Mademoiselle," said Madame, "*vraiment*—this Olympus is such a charming place we will not return to earth,
I think, but send Mercury for a plate of ambrosia and
a cup of nectar, and remain to admire these gods and
goddesses so beautiful."

"Miss Rory," called out Mary Ellen, who, with the
cooing Bluebell over her shoulder, had joined the party

a few minutes before, "you've left off your petticoat, so don't deny it. Come down at once, you know I won't have you playing amongst those nasty funerally-looking cypresses!"

To the delight of some of the party this divinity on the pedestal stuck out a pink tongue at Mary Ellen, which made Cassandra murmur something which certainly was not blank verse to the statue, and glide away once more.

Away she sped to the woods where the pines were thick and tall and the shadows deep under the beech-trees, and then things began to happen. A sudden silvery laugh made every one jump round, though there was nothing to be seen but a wood-pecker climbing up a tree and peeping round and round in his curious way.

Then came a sound very sweet and elusive—one could not be sure if it were a flute far away, or the gentle ringing of wind-bells among the trees, and while everybody stood listening, a harsh, discordant, rather terrible voice called suddenly from the pine-trees, which made Pauline and several other nervous ones nearly jump out of their skins.

"Do you know I rather believe Pan is about," said Wendy, smiling.

Then Pandora called out; "There he is; I say, how jolly!"

There in a little fern-grove, on the grassy knoll before a tall beech-tree, sat Jill, or rather Pan, for her small mischievous face against the background of greenery, her dark silky hair wreathed with leaves, and her expression of almost fiendish merriment was the very Pan of one's imagination. She was half-draped in a goat-skin, and in her brown, slender fingers she held a flute of reeds.

She never moved a muscle, and when Cassandra had

related her history they were all led away to the Isle of Ææa.

There was a tiny lake in the grounds of Idle Pines, the pride of the girls' hearts, for it had a real island in the middle of it—certainly not much bigger than a good-sized table-cloth, but big enough to be the scene of many romantic adventures. On it stood three small pine-trees which had formed the walls of many a wigwam, fairy palace, Greek temple or anything else desired in their imaginative games.

Gay-coloured silken curtains were hung between them roofed with green boughs, representing the entrance to the palace of the lovely sorceress Circe, on the Isle of Ææa.

Cassandra had taken an immense amount of trouble over the arrangement of this last scene, and Julie, in flaming robes, holding a golden cup—really gold, for Rory had provided it from a cabinet of precious antiques in the library—and drugged with the draught of enchantment, was to burst in all her beauty upon the sight of the beholders when Cassandra drew aside the curtain.

A bridge led to the Isle, so fragile that Wendy trembled for the safety of Aunt Sally, and the juniors hoped rather wickedly that somebody *would* provide the next item on the programme by falling into the lake.

But Cassandra crossed the tiny bridge, followed by the whole party, and no sooner had they landed on the charmed shores of Ææa than they heard strange and unaccountable sounds that could hardly be called enchanting.

"Well, I must say," cried Laurette, "if I had been Ulysses' sailors I should have gone the other way round when I heard that noise."

"I never knew goddesses *grunted*," said Pauline. Cassandra, puzzled and a little anxious, unrolled her scroll and began:

"And now the wind-god mighty Æolus
Ulysses' ship swept to the fairy Isle
Ææa, where dwelt the lovely Circe,
Enchantress who charmed with melody
More sweet than songs of lark or flute of Pan.
And Ulysses sent forth Eurylochus
With the good ship's crew, for they were hungry.
And Ææa offered fruit more purple
Than the robes of kings to thirsty men.
Upon her shores there stood the golden house
Of Circe,—ravished by the sweetness
Of her voice, they stood spellbound and——"

Drawing back the curtain from the palace door where the enchantress was supposed to be singing while weaving her magic spell, Cassandra gave a gasp of horrified bewilderment, and after the first moment of astonishment the whole school burst into peals of laughter!

Instead of a lovely sorceress singing a melody enchanting enough to turn strong men into foolish slaves, there lay Circe, the big, prize black sow of Idle Pines.

She wore a Greek tunic draped over her hairy shoulders, and a chaplet of flowers fell over one flapping ear.

Furious with indignation, Cassandra would have liked to fling the absent Circe into the lake—and Pan too, for it was easy to guess that he had not looked so fiendishly merry in the wood for nothing.

But she had not been brought up by Wendy and browsed on Greek heroes all her life for nothing, so she dropped the curtain and said quietly, "I'm sorry, but *somebody* evidently thinks that prize pigs will amuse you more than Greek statuary—and it seems as though she is right," and giving a disdainful look to the laughing girls, she turned away.

Leaving her pupils to Madame, Wendy followed the despondent Greek maiden quietly and said, "My darling

child, don't look so tragic. It was too bad, of course, to
spoil such a charming idea, but schoolgirls will be
schoolgirls."

"Horrid little toads! I might have known they would
spoil everything—and how *dare* they do such a thing
when they knew you and Madame and everybody else
would be there?"

"They probably felt dull at a school where there are
no punishments or impositions, and want to see how
I shall deal with a crime of this sort; well, they *shall*
see."

She looked at Cassandra tenderly; for she knew so
well how she felt—tired and disheartened, and longing
to get away to a room of her own for a little of the
solitude she loved and missed so much, now that Idle
Pines was full of girls.

"Now, just because you are named Cassandra, please
don't prophesy that my Idea is going to fail," she
said. "Would you like to slip away to the library, and
have Mary Ellen bring your tea in the orange parrot
teapot?"

"What a duck you are, Wendy," said Cassandra grate-
fully. "I feel I simply couldn't stand a school tea this
afternoon, and I'd rather not see those little wretches
until I've cooled down," and she went off to be cheered
up by the orange parrot teapot, and to be petted by
Mary Ellen.

Julie and Jill appeared at tea-time trying to look innocent and unconcerned; but to their astonishment, and
a little to their chagrin too, not a single allusion was
made to their dramatic tableau.

Wendy and the staff ignored them entirely, and Laurette
and Penelope merely looked contemptuous.

"Get ready to be summoned to the library," said Jill
after tea. "I say, this is one of the times I shouldn't
miss being back in the 'No Rules' school; they didn't

believe in rows there, you know, they were too busy worrying about your dreams and things."

But no summons came; they were still completely ignored by their elders, and Cassandra passed them disdainfully.

Before bed-time they approached her boldly.

" I say, Cassandra, I suppose you're fearfully ratty about the trick we played, but——"

"No, I'm not; it was just what I expected."

"Expected!"

"Yes. Of course, a person who has been a Pierrot would think it amusing to dress up a pig, and I dare say Jill was a Christy Minstrel or something of that sort at one of those dozen schools she has sampled."

Cassandra passed on and left the two heroines distinctly troubled.

After enduring three days of chilly politeness from their elders, the Circe episode still ignored, Jill vowed she could stand it no longer.

"It's all very well to do outrageous things and get in a row about it and take the consequences," she announced; "it's like confessing your sins and paying your debts, and when you've done it it's finished with—but this is too awful. Let's go to Miss Wendell and ask her to shut as up for a week, or give us ten thousand lines or something, just as any other head mistress would do, except at that cranky 'No Rules' school where the kids were all such little horrors."

Julie, who also felt she would like a nice old-fashioned punishment and have done with the whole affair, agreed, and they marched off to Miss Wendell at once.

Jill was spokeswoman, and began: "Miss Wendell, do *please* punish us or lecture us or something for what we did about Circe."

"Why should I do that, Jill?"

"Because it was such a silly thing to do, and, anyhow, you didn't like it, so we ought to be punished."

"But you know just as well as I know that it was a silly thing to do, as well as showing very bad manners and unkindness to an animal. Nobody appreciates fun more than I do; but practical jokes of that sort are usually only done by rather stupid people."

Jill flushed scarlet—"guilty of bad manners, silliness and cruelty to animals"—*she*, who always tried to be polite and thought herself rather a clever person, and *adored* animals! Julie looked wretched too.

"Oh, Miss Wendell, don't say that, please. I hate rude people, and Circe didn't mind being taken to the island, really she didn't."

"If Circe was not hurt, Cassandra was. You amused yourselves actually at her expense, not to speak of your rudeness to myself, and Madame and the rest."

"I know, it was *awful*; that's why we want you to do something really horrid to us, please."

"No, Jill, I told you all that I don't believe in continual punishments; it's like trying to cure a sick person, who only needs a healthy open-air life, with frequent doses of medicine. We are all going to see how happily we can live together for a year; but those who cannot conform to the rules must go—to a school where they can have as many inattention marks, order marks, impositions and punishments as they like."

This was terrible. Here was Miss Wendell telling them they would probably be expelled before the end of the year for rudeness and lack of intelligence. Jill, who had always left a school at once if she disliked it, and was happy away from Moti for the first time in her life because everything was so jolly at Idle Pines.

"But, Miss Wendell, do you really mean we are to punish ourselves?" asked Julie.

"I think it would not only do you good, but show everybody you feel you were entirely in the wrong."

Downcast, they both retreated, for it wasn't at all pleasant to be made entirely responsible for their own actions.

"We might ask every one to the lake-side to watch us scourge ourselves with knotted cords near the scene of our crime," suggested Jill, who liked dramatic effects.

But Julie objected to knotted cords, and also to Jill's idea of fasting from jam and cakes for a whole week.

"Miss Wendell believes in the punishment fitting the crime," she said; "besides, knotted cords and things are so monkish."

It was Aunt Sally who gave them an idea for self-punishment at last, for they heard her in the stable-yard, loudly rating Joe for the disgraceful state of the pigsties, while he retorted that he already had enough to do for a dozen men.

Julie looked at Jill, and Jill looked at Julie, and her face went pale. "They're so horribly smelly," she objected.

"I know," said Julie, becoming enthusiastic; "that will show them we are not proud and really *love* Circe, and it will be rather thrilling too, like Hercules clearing out the Augean stables, you know—that will please that little owl of a Cassandra."

"But when can we do it?" asked Jill.

"To-morrow, while the others bathe. We'll have to miss that, which is sickening, but it can't be helped."

So the matter was settled, and the next morning at eleven o'clock, when the whole school had departed to enjoy a cool bathe, the imitators of the immortal Hercules began to cleanse the Circean pigsties. But, unlike Hercules, they had no rivers from which to dig a trench for a rush of water to do the cleansing; so Jill fetched the hose-pipe, and before many minutes they were both far wetter than their comrades in the sea. Burning with enthusiasm, they did their Herculean task thoroughly, scrubbing out the troughs until Julie declared she would eat out of them herself, and removing all the litter and replacing it with sweet dry bracken fetched from the pine-wood. Then the lovely Circe herself was cleansed, her back scrubbed vigorously, and because Jill was afraid she was still a little "smelly," she rushed and fetched a bottle of eau-de-Cologne—one of Moti's gifts—and gave her a final scented bath. Everything spotless, they washed out their overalls at the pump and hung them on the gorse bushes to dry, rushed to the bath-room for a hasty cold bath, and were down in readiness to receive the bathing party.

"Why on earth didn't you come?" asked Pandora, "the sea was glorious and——"

"Miss Wendell, will you please come and see something?" asked Julie politely.

"Of course I will—where is it?"

"In the palace of Circe," said Jill, and immediately the whole party rushed after Wendy.

Circe, shining with cleanliness, lay snoring on her sweet litter, in a sty fragrant with eau-de-Cologne.

"Why, how splendid! Who did it?" asked Wendy, giving the two girls a look which told them plainly she understood and that everything was forgiven and forgotten.

"*We* did," said Julie and Jill together. "We have cleansed the pigsties—like Hercules, you know," and they glanced at Cassandra, who said, "Well, I do think that was awfully decent of you."

Aunt Sally, wearing a green mackintosh bathing-cap, gazed at the pigsty in admiration.

"If they can do a job like that once, they can do it again," she said; "we'll make swineherds of 'em; I can't get that Joe to touch 'em."

This was a nice reward for their labours, and they

both looked so wretched that Wendy said hastily, "No, it's Joe's work, and there are other things we want Julie and Jill to do, though it is splendid to think they *can* clean out pigsties in an emergency, and next time we show Circe we must ask them to perform her toilet before she starts."

Afterwards, Wendy said to Madame and Miss Dillon, "There! you see I *am* right. Those two children have cleared their own consciences, and feel perfectly happy in consequence. I believe children love discipline really, unless they have no backbone or grit. I don't think those two girls will hurt anybody's feelings again without thinking a little, and the delicate way they tried to please Cassandra shows that she succeeded in interesting them in Greek mythology better than she thought, which will make her happy, too."

And Madame said, "*Tiens! Ces Anglais!* To learn a moral lesson from *un cochon* to me seems a little *drôle*, my friend!"

CHAPTER 9

THE NEW DOOMSDAY BOOK

THE days flew by happily at Idle Pines.

Wendy had a genius for making every one enthusiastic about work as well as play. Although she held the reins firmly she seldom used the whip, and before the term was half over she was adored and had become Wendy to the whole school, which did not cause her to lose her dignity in the least.

The girls rose early, and although there was some grumbling at Aunt Sally's tasks, every one really enjoyed those lovely morning hours in the garden, and there was the keenest competition among the vegetable and flower growers for the finest specimens. In fact, Rory erected all the family umbrellas, including Jane's best pearl-handled one, over her pet lettuces during the drought, and Meg gave up her evening recreation to snail-catching.

Eve and Penelope were the head milkmaids, and Pandora, Jill, and Rory usually attended to the ponies and fed the cats and dogs. Isobel and Julie had the care of the calves, and Cassandra and several of the younger girls were responsible for the poultry.

But when all these lessons and duties were over they went for long rides and rambles in the Forest, played games, bathed and found time to make clothes for Bluebell, now the most wonderful baby ever owned by thirty-four adoring godmothers.

Mary Leslie was Mistress of Her Majesty's Robes, and never had a baby a more varied and dainty wardrobe. She had cosy knitted coats and caps, and her best frocks and her cot cover of white lamb's-wool were embroidered with bluebells.

"She's a frightfully expensive hobby," said Jill, "and we needn't have kicked up that rumpus about Rule IV after all, as we certainly shall never have any money to spare for sweets from the village shop with this person to clothe and educate."

They bathed and dressed her, prepared her food and washed her bottles scrupulously, and also refrained from jogging her up and down while she partook of them, for Jessie Mills's plain-spoken advice was not forgotten.

Bluebell rewarded them by loving everybody, although it was true that she enjoyed pulling Jill's hair the most and Rory was her favourite Court Jester.

There was no dullness in the daily school routine, for Wendy, determined to make her pupils capable, was constantly springing all sorts of surprise tasks upon them.

Sometimes she would order six girls into the kitchen to cook a plain dinner, without help or advice from Jane; and Penelope, the dreamy, and Isobel, the timid, were forced to wake up and be practical and bold when they were sent to choose and buy materials for Bluebell's outfit.

There was a good-tempered rivalry between the four patrols, which kept them all busy and out of mischief. Mary Leslie, who had clever fingers, set her seven to making things for the school Fancy Fair to be held later on. They made wonderful bead necklaces out of paper and macaroni, and dyed them in bright colours, and they also made toy dogs, ducks, penguins and elephants, all stuffed with the sawdust from the big pine tree Dorothy was sawing into winter logs.

Isobel was in despair over her seven, until Wendy suggested they should all be still-room maids, and dry herbs and lavender for household use, and make scents, and pot-pourri and cordials to cure the school's aches and pains.

"I should *love* it," cried Isobel, and she pored over the old herbal books in the library with such success that before long every one envied the "topping" things done by the fourth patrol.

Eve bought a book on Scout lore and turned her pro-tégées into such enthusiasts that the whole school found it rather useful having seven people in search of a daily good deed!

"They'll have used up everything soon," prophesied Jill with a grin, "and then I suppose Pauline will think it a good deed to give a mouse to the cat, like the Boy Scout! Pandora, my child, I can see you are dying to get a good action off your mind for to-day, so sing out those declensions for me while I write them out, there's an angel."

It was Pauline who disgraced Eve's patrol.

From the moment she had arrived at Idle Pines she had been a girl with a grievance, and the despair of the over-anxious Pandora.

She resented the open windows, the early rising, and Aunt Sally's commands; but most of all she resented not being admitted into Jill's set.

All her efforts to become really friendly with the fascinating Jill and her little circle were in vain, for Pauline was a spoil-sport as well as a grumbler, and that was the reason Pandora and Rory always ignored her frequent hints to be invited to the Sanctuary.

Knowing Jill's love of mischief, Pauline decided that the way to win her favour was to play some amusing and rather daring practical joke on the school, proving that she also had a love of adventure.

She racked her brains to think of something, for she was not clever and her imagination found it difficult to soar beyond apple-pie beds and booby-traps.

Then, suddenly, she had a brilliant idea; at least, Pauline considered it brilliant.

Cricket was not *the* game at Idle Pines, although the girls often played it. They were good tennis-players, and Dorothy was trying to make them keen on archery.

She was an enthusiast on the subject of classical and folk-dancing, and four times a week her pupils danced barefooted on the big lawn, or else in country frocks and buckled shoes they practised the dances seen on village greens when the Merry Monarch reigned, or played old English games till bedtime.

Pauline had twisted her ankle slightly; just seriously enough to prevent her using it much for a few days, and this was why she thought it would be extremely amusing to scatter on the velvety smoothness of the lawn some prickly holly leaves.

She hugged herself with joy at the thought of the yells of the injured and Dorothy's wrath at the interruptions in the lesson.

That evening, for once, Pauline did not dog the footsteps of Jill's followers. She hastened to the shrubbery instead, where holly leaves abounded.

She brushed up the leaves quickly into a big basket and carried it off to the deserted lawn, and there, with a patience which would have surprised her teachers, she sprinkled the prickly leaves in all directions, tipping the rest of the litter under the cedar tree.

It happened that on that particular evening old Miss Caird paid an unexpected visit to Idle Pines.

Miss Caird lived at the Manor House and was a sort of fairy godmother to the villagers, for ever racking her brains to make them as happy as her rescued cats and dogs, and the worn-out horses that she bought and pensioned out in her stables and paddocks.

She was fond of Wendy and the girls because of their

devotion to animals, and though she was old and lame she often came in her bath-chair to pay them a visit.

She sat under the big cedar tree with Wendy, ready to enjoy her first sight of classical dancing, and Pauline sat near, virtuously mending one of Bluebell's socks.

Gladys Shaw was the first victim. If there was a rabbit-hole about, Gladys always stumbled into it; she had never been known not to step into a puddle, so naturally her toes instantly danced on to the prickliest holly leaf.

She uttered such a piercing yell that every dancer stood stock still, and Dorothy, anxious that her pupils should do her credit before a stranger, asked wrathfully, "What *is* the matter? Gladys, how dare you stop the dance in this way?"

"It's a thorn in my toe," wept Gladys. "I do think——"

"A thorn!" cried Dorothy scornfully—"don't talk nonsense. Mavis and Joyce swept the lawn as usual this morning. Carry on at once, girls."

Fortunately, Miss Caird, very busy telling Wendy about some village scheme, and slightly deaf, hardly noticed the interruption.

The Will-o'-the-Wisp dance continued, but, alas! the dancers looked more like flying kangaroos in distress than wraiths of the mist, for there were new victims in all directions, trying to stifle their shrieks like true Spartans, so that no disgrace should fall on the class in the presence of Miss Caird.

Suddenly Meg burst into tears and Gladys gave another yell, just as Jill murmured to Pandora, "I say, I feel like a hedgehog; I'd like to know what ass thought *this* would be funny."

Pauline, overhearing, began to have qualms. The faces of her victims boded ill for the practical joker, and the fascinating Jill seemed more disgusted than amused.

"Stand still," ordered Dorothy, and Laurette cried,

"It's no good; we really have tried to go on, Dorothy, but I don't feel inclined to hop about on thorns another second," and she lifted up her foot and examined the sole tenderly, and the rest of the Will-o'-the-Wisps followed her example.

Dorothy inspected the lawn wrathfully. It was quite true.

"Run and change into shoes and bells as fast as you can," she ordered; "we'll give Miss Caird some country dances."

But before anybody could obey orders, Isobel suddenly collapsed in a dazed, frightened way and said, "Something's bitten me. Oh, it's a *viper*!"

Almost as she spoke the Forest-bred Rory flew to her, and, kneeling down, instantly sucked the tiny red spot on Isobel's foot. Then Pandora and Jill came to life and, pursuing the viper gliding wickedly over the grass, Pandora killed it swiftly with a croquet mallet which was fortunately at hand.

Gladys Shaw's scream of horror at the sight of the snake brought Wendy on the scene, and she immediately sent Penelope indoors for brandy and Condy's fluid, and the wound was treated at once, while she soothed Isobel, still white and trembling, by telling her Forest folk were used to vipers, and if remedies were applied quickly there was nothing at all to fear.

"But where *could* it have come from, Wendy?" demanded Rory. "We never see them on the lawn, only in garden rubbish and things like that; suppose it had bitten one of the angels!"

Julie, prowling round, suddenly announced, "Why, here's a heap of litter—dry leaves and things. I suppose the person who sowed holly leaves all over the grass threw that down too."

Pauline shuddered. After all, snakes were more dangerous than thorns, and twice already she had seen

Dorothy glance in her direction suspiciously, and she distinctly heard Jill say to Pandora, "It's that ass, Pauline, I feel sure; it's just the sort of silly joke she would think amusing."

In fact, the whole of her brilliant idea seemed to have come to grief as far as she was concerned. All it had done was to show off Pandora, Jill, and Rory as heroines— Wendy had praised them for presence of mind—and Pauline was farther away than ever from becoming friendly with the most popular girl in the school.

To make matters worse, Dorothy, after a few words to Wendy, sauntered up to Pauline and said, "Oh, Pauline, you can't dance to-night, of course, but I don't want your ankle to get stiff through sitting about. Some very silly person thought it funny to scatter holly leaves over the lawn; it's really too stupid to bother about, as Miss Wendell says, but we want *you* to take a little exercise and pick them all up while the others are dancing. Oh, and clear away all that litter too, please, snake bites *are* sometimes dangerous, you know."

It was in vain the lazy Pauline remonstrated and limped on her injured ankle. Dorothy's command must be obeyed; in fact, picking up hundreds of holly leaves while the others gaily danced was the only reward Pauline received for trying to play a daring practical joke.

Miss Caird, who had been politely entertained by a few senior girls while all this was happening, now sat and watched with astonishment and delight a group of morris-dancers jingling their bells on the sunlit lawn.

"Well, my dear," she said to Wendy, "this *is* a treat. I haven't been in a girls' school for over fifty years, and that was when I was a pupil at a Brighton boarding-school for young ladies. Oh, my dear! you should have seen me. Not a day older than that pretty little maid over there, and skirts down to my feet; it wasn't polite to show your legs in those days, though why they should be a secret I can't imagine. Our feet had to look like 'little mice peeping in and out,' as the poet said, if you wanted to be genteel; and I'm sure I wore more petticoats over them than these young ladies own between them!

"And the buckram, crammed into our neckbands and stuffed into our bodices, not to speak of the whalebone down our poor spines, and Miss Jaggs coming into the dormitory every morning to see if we were laced tightly.

"We used to sit all day, answering Magnall's 'Questions,' and doing endless copies and practising duets, and never played games except croquet on Saturday afternoons. We talked about nothing except new crochet-stitches, our clothes, and what would happen when we 'came out,' and instead of dancing in the open air with all our limbs free and bells on our toes, we had lessons in deportment and danced slow quadrilles, and thought the polka terribly exciting. And all the time, my dear, I was burning to kick away my petticoats, and dance and sing, and speak when I wasn't spoken to, like these lucky girls. But, dear me, my poor mother would have fainted if she had seen a young lady playing hockey."

"Would you like them to sing to you?" asked Wendy.

"Very much, my dear. I haven't enjoyed myself so much watching young people for years."

She beamed like a nice old fairy-godmother while the girls sang and danced "Come, Lassies and Lads," then she clapped her hands and cried, "Now, listen to me, dears. You know you are all Miss Wendell's children —and lucky children, too—but I'm god-mother to half the lassies and lads in this village, and feel quite like a foolish old granny about them all.

"Now who can think of a plan to keep the creatures amused and teach them something? If a little maid in this school can make a good practical suggestion, I will reward her by giving something to the school.

"They had better all write essays on ' How to Brighten Village Life,'" suggested Wendy, "and you could adopt any idea in them you think good."

"Excellent; let's have 'em as soon as you can, my dears, and then you'll see what a generous old woman I can be when anybody helps me with *my* children!"

She then departed, leaving a rather excited group of girls behind her, for Wendy's ambition was realised already, and nearly every girl felt enthusiastic about the school's welfare, and was delighted at the idea of winning a gift for its improvement.

"Now, listen to me, children," said Wendy. "I suggest that as we are such a united community, we shall all give our ideas when we have thought of them, and let the most literary among you write an essay about them for Miss Caird; that will mean that everybody helps to benefit the school."

This was agreed to be a good plan, and Jill suggested that Cassandra should be the "literary one" on the spot.

"But I haven't got an idea," objected Pauline, always injured.

"Couldn't we have a class for them on Sunday afternoons?" said Meg, who had been brought up on old-fashioned books and pined to be a benefactress to a row of starched village children—"not too goody-goody—just to teach them how to behave and all that."

"They *know* how to behave," cried Rory indignantly, and Pandora said, "And Miss Caird wants us to improve their minds; doesn't she, Wendy?"

"She wants to keep them happily amused by using their brains, fingers, and imaginations, I expect. We will all talk it over in the holidays, and when you come back in September we will compare notes."

Time had rushed by with such rapid footsteps that the term was nearly over, and with the exception of Eve, Jill, and Nancy, who was having two small sisters to stay with her while their parents were in Norway, the girls were all going home in a few days.

Eve stayed because she preferred a country life at Idle Pines to spending a month at a fashionable seaside resort with her family. Jill couldn't leave, and even Cassandra didn't mind Jill, although she longed to have the house to herself more than any of them; but it was a terrible blow to everybody when it was announced that Gladys Shaw's brother had developed scarlet fever, and she must remain as a holiday boarder too.

Pauline was considered the nuisance of the school because of her perpetual grumbling; but Gladys really was the most unpopular girl at Idle Pines.

"She'll spoil everything," wailed Rory; "Nancy is bad enough."

Jill was indignant, too; for though she made a point of being friends with everybody, Gladys had offended her by saying that a particularly thrilling chapter of "Lost and Found," related one night in "Somnus," was "dull."

Nancy's sisters, Peggy and Barbara, twins aged ten, were not so patronising as Meg, and came so plainly prepared to enjoy themselves that Rory was secretly rather glad to see them, especially as they preferred bicycles to ponies, so that Jackyboy would be really her own for six whole weeks, for Gladys had her own pony.

When everybody but Aunt Sally had departed, things seemed very quiet and strange, and the cats and dogs lost no time in taking up their cool quarters on the chairs on the veranda. To Cassandra's delight, she was given a holiday bedroom all to herself, and the younger girls were sent up to Sparta for change of scene and air.

"And it's just in time," said Jill; "those poppies were beginning to get on my nerves; besides, it's jolly up here and we can have lots of fun."

"Oh, yes," cried Peggy and Barbara rapturously; "pillow fights and things."

"*Pillow* fights!" said Gladys scornfully; "for goodness' sake, let's do something exciting."

The first morning of the holidays, Pandora, Jill, and Rory cautiously made their escape to the Sanctuary after kidnapping Bluebell from the nursery, not forgetting to set Mary Ellen's heart at rest by writing, "The child is safe and will return to earth ere the sun sets—Three of *Them*," which they pinned to Bluebell's pincushion.

"The little wretches," said Penelope when she discovered it, for she had planned to have the cuddlesome Bluebell all to herself that morning.

But the little wretches were enjoying every moment, and in half an hour the Sanctuary was completely turned out under the pine-trees, where Bluebell hung from a branch as happily as a fat little papoose.

Rory washed and ironed the curtains. Jill scrubbed the floors, and Pandora lit the fire and made a blackcurrant pie and boiled potatoes and peas for dinner.

By two o'clock everything was in order again, and the house completely rearranged by Jill, whose artistic ideas were generously acknowledged by Pandora and Rory. Then, taking turns to swing Bluebell on their backs, they slipped down to the cliffs and gathered early blackberries, which were made into jam at once and eaten with hot potato cakes.

At six o'clock they returned, and were met by Eve and Penelope, who seized Bluebell indignantly and marched her off to bed.

They escaped Mary Ellen, and returned to Sparta, where they hastily removed their rags and all traces of the day's work.

"I say, just look at my knees," cried Jill, rubbing her chafed skin tenderly. "I believe I'm in for housemaid's knees as well as a decline; what awful news for Moti!"

"Enjoyed yourselves?" Wendy asked pleasantly.

"Rather," said the runaways, still a little sheepish. "I say, Wendy, where are the others?"

"Getting ready for supper, I suppose. I took them all over to the Fête at Westchurch; it was a pity you disappeared before it was settled," and Wendy strolled away.

"The Fête! *what* a sell!" groaned Pandora, for though it had been heaven in the Sanctuary away from the tiresome Gladys, fêtes were run with stalls, and roundabouts and coco-nut-shies.

"I should have thought my housemaid's knee enough punishment," said Jill bitterly, and Rory wailed, "And there would be gipsies and caravans. Well, if we ever *are* impolite, Wendy always lets us know what she thinks about it."

It was annoying to see Gladys in her laciest petticoat, and Nancy and her sisters arrive at the supper-table, all carrying coco-nuts knocked down by themselves.

The punishment was complete, and the culprits showed their penitence by inviting everybody to come and see the spick and span Sanctuary.

But Wendy said, "No; you've been racing about all day. I want you all to come under the cedar and listen to my new idea."

Wendy's ideas usually proving exciting, everybody accepted this invitation with alacrity, and Rory said, "Well, *do* be quick, Wendy."

"I'm going to write a new Doomsday Book."

"A new *Doomsday* Book! But why?"

"Because it would be so nice for the school to own one all about Hampshire, you know: its history, old customs, proverbs, local sayings and dialects, landmarks, and the country names for the moors, lanes, and dykes that are used now—that's why I call it a *new* Doomsday Book, the sort that Welsh school-children are beginning to write about Wales."

"But, Wendy, Doomsday Books don't sound a bit exciting for the holidays," Rory looked mournful, and Gladys murmured, "Catch *me* writing history-books."

"But one doesn't sit down in a room and write the history of a county. Wouldn't it be exciting to have a caravan, and set off on our travels to explore the Forest and make friends with the foresters, and see if we can't find out where the honey buzzard and the hoopoe nest —the Forest is wonderful for birds—to record in our very own Doomsday Book?"

Jill sprang up, and Pandora and Rory flew to Wendy and screamed, "Do you *really* mean travel in a caravan, Wendy, darling?"

"Not if you throttle me; but if you don't, and we can get a caravan, and you all like my idea, we can start next week and begin to write our book as we jog along."

"Do you mean *all* write it?" asked Nancy, rather awestruck.

"Every one can help."

"But it would take *ages* to write a book of that sort," said Cassandra.

"Years, I should think, but we could begin it."

"It would be heavenly in a caravan," said Jill. "When shall we start?"

"When we can find a caravan; I have heard of one."

"Oh, Wendy, write *now*." Pandora never could wait, and would certainly have opened the wonderful Box as the mythological Pandora did, as Wendy often said.

"Very well; go to bed, and I'll write now."

The juniors departed to feast on coco-nut and discuss the caravan journey with joy, all but Gladys, who said she "hated this everlasting picnicking" and she'd rather go to Hastings for a holiday than traipes about like a gipsy in the Forest.

"You can be the sort of gipsy that wears velvet dresses, beads, and feathers on your hat," suggested Jill; "I think it will be gorgeous."

"I wonder if we'll take Bluebell," said Pan.

"Of course we will." Rory was indignant. "Just as if we should be so mean as to leave the youngest-girl-in-the-school behind!"

"I say, Rory," said Jill, "if we're going into the Forest with Bluebell, we'll jolly well have to look out that *They* don't walk off with her again!" a remark which made the Hastings-loving Gladys say, "I call all this silly talk about fairies absolute *rot*," and put an extra dab of powder on her nose.

CHAPTER 10

TREE TOPS

But Wendy wouldn't hear of the school baby caravanning. She said they must take the luck of the road about food, and that the nursery was a more suitable place for cutting teeth than the New Forest. Bluebell's mothers were disappointed, especially Rory, who said people in caravans always sat on the steps with babies in their laps.

"There won't be any laps," said Wendy; "we must all tramp. It will do us good, and the caravan will be quite loaded enough with such a big tent to carry."

Aunt Sally had no patience with the idea. "Why on earth you want to go mooning into the Forest after plants and caterpillars and butterflies and quaint sayings I can't imagine," she said. "If it's caterpillars you want, there are plenty waiting to be picked off the currant-bushes—don't expect any black-currants next year. And as for Hampshire dialect, that Joe will stand and talk by the hour while somebody else does his work for him. Don't ask me to hope you will have nice weather, because I shan't. I hope it will pour for a fortnight; I'd rather see the blight washed off the beans than you enjoy yourselves."

But nobody minded Aunt Sally, and when the caravan was left at Idle Pines by its owner, who preferred home-life for a fortnight, even Gladys acknowledged it was a "perfectly super one."

It was painted a dull grey, which went well with the tree trunks and the Forest's wide spaces, and the pails and water-cans that jingled beneath it were of a vivid green, with "Tree Tops" painted on them in white letters. "Tree Tops" was painted on the little door too, and it seemed a delightful name for a caravan.

To make things still more delightful, Wendy said they might all dress as they pleased for the journey, so long as each one was provided with a raincoat and strong shoes.

The four ponies, Snow Queen, Night, Redskin, and Jackyboy, were taken to pull the caravan, which was a heavy one, and the four dogs went, of course.

They started off on a brilliantly sunny August morning, and Jane, who was in a gloomy mood owing to the oven being "in one of his nasty tempers," prophesied rain before noon, as all her corns were "twingeing up to her shoulder-blades like."

"And at the first drop, you put on your raincoat, Miss Rory," commanded Mary Ellen; "for begin the autumn with a cold in the house I can't and won't."

"If it rains again before Doomsday I shall be surprised," said Aunt Sally. "For goodness' sake start, for that Joe won't do a stroke till he's done gaping at you all, and the sooner you get off, the sooner you'll be back to help with the watering, I hope."

As Wendy said, they must be *real* travellers and take the luck of the road. They carried nothing but their next meal of brown bread and butter, Eve's cream cheeses, raspberry tarts, ripe gooseberries and milk.

They took the broad forest road which stretches like a wide moor from Forest Lodge, ablaze with scented, bee-haunted heather. Around the shallow pools the forest ponies stood with their clumsy, woolly little foals —"angels" that Pandora, Rory, and Jill longed to adopt.

Then they turned away from the broad highway to the deep coolness of the great beech-trees that spread their sheltering green arms over lovely little Burley, with its ancient holly-woods that stood when kings hunted in the Forest long ago, and the good men of Burley presented them with snow-white deer-hounds for the royal chase.

With one accord every one agreed that Burley must be the first camp; because the woods were so thick and glorious, and their deep glades the very place to see *Them* if you kept awake all night, as Rory argued. There were splendid open spaces too, golden with tawny marsh grass and silver with waving "moor-silk," as Mary Ellen so prettily called the cotton grass.

"It looks like a giant patchwork quilt," said Rory, looking at the stretch of country below her; "all yellow and purple and green and brown and red; and aren't holly-woods lovely and cool and rustly and pixie-ish?"

There was pasture for the ponies, too, and Pandora discovered a cottage inhabited by a delightful person, who seemed willing to provide endless information for the new Doomsday Book. She wore a pink print gown, and her old face was as crinkled as a winter apple, and anybody could have guessed her name was "Rose," even if it hadn't been written on the silver brooch which fastened the white tucker at her neck. Her garden was full of pink cabbage roses and holly-hocks, and the handle of her pump was polished till it shone like silver, and the moon was no brighter than the row of tin pails outside her kitchen door. In her red-tiled outer kitchen a black kettle hung suspended by a chain over an open hearth where a wood-fire burned, for what forester is going to burn coal and mar the spotlessness of her best kitchen in summer-time, when wood and pine-cones are to be gathered round her door?

"When the Whitsun bosses is out we puts out the fire in here regular," she explained to Wendy; "and when the holly berries turns yellow, the master he goes back to his arm-chair there in the corner and takes his comfort."

"What on earth is a Whitsun boss?" asked Eve. "It

sounds quite feudal. Is he a lord of the manor who orders them to put out their fires?"

The country-bred Penelope explained that "Whitsun bosses" are the big moon-like flowers of the wild guelder-rose, which cover the hedges in Hampshire and Dorset at Whitsuntide, and Nancy industriously made a note of it.

This fresh-faced old Rose of the forest was willing that they should pick her ripe gooseberries, and shook her head when Wendy wished to pay, saying they were welcome to them and also to some of the big broad beans in her garden—"the best in the Forest, because the master knew that if you set the seeds on the shortest day you'd get good beans on the longest; and what's nicer than a dish of beans and bacon when you're hungry?"

She told them that Sarah Wise at the farm at the turn of the lane would let them have butter and eggs and milk, and Forest honey, too, if the young ladies liked sweet things.

"What's the name of the lane?" asked Gladys, thinking this a good opportunity to get her contribution to the new Doomsday Book.

"They do call it the End of Paradise, Miss, where it turns down by the hollies; and beyond that, where the land goes up and down so beautiful, the folks round here calls the Gates of Heaven."

"Oh, Wendy, isn't it glorious?" cried Rory, when Sarah Wise had supplied the foraging party with bread and honey and milk and butter, and they were all enjoying this feast on the heather, which stretched like a soft purple carpet before the caravan; "whoever thought we should ever camp outside the Gates of Heaven?"

"And hardly any midges now we're away from the trees," said Jill. "And that's *so* comforting, because there oughtn't to be any midges in Paradise."

Sarah Wise's two black sows, Susy and Sally, and five geese came to tea, but nobody objected to that except Gladys, who also declared that she couldn't see any fun in fetching water from Rose's pump for washing up the tea-things.

It was the greatest fun getting ready for the night; though it really was not like night at all with a moon swinging like a great silver lantern over the Forest, and the only darkness lying in the shadows of the holly trees, which stood round the caravan like armed soldiers, their sober, prickly old heads crowned with yellow-tinted wreaths of honeysuckle.

There were four berths inside "Tree Tops," occupied by Rory, Nancy, Barbara, and Peggy, and the back of the caravan let down in a most ingenious way, making room for three hammocks to be swung for Pandora, Jill, and Gladys. The tent was pitched near, though Wendy and the older girls preferred to swing their hammocks in the open on such a lovely summer night.

Pandora, Jill, and Rory had secretly decided to keep awake all night to see what happened in this mysterious, moonlit forest when the world was asleep; but, alas! almost before their heads had touched their pine-scented pillows, they were sleeping as soundly as Susy and Sally near the coolness of the duck-pond in Sarah Wise's yard.

At about one o'clock a tawny owl shrieked out its startling cry of "hullabaloo! hullabaloo!" just as a Forest pony strolled up with her week-old foal to see what a caravan party looked like; and Gladys awoke with a shriek more fearful than the owls, saying she would *not* sleep in a place where mad people screamed and horses breathed on you.

She was comforted by Cassandra's hammock, which was near Wendy's protecting presence, and Pandora, Jill, and Rory took the opportunity during the disturbance to slip out of bed and experience the joys of rolling on the heather of a moonlit forest in the middle of the night, and the "ordinaries" slept soundly through it all.

In the morning Eve and the little girls fetched water for the baths, Pandora, Gladys, and Jill shook up the bedding and spread it out to air, and Wendy and Penelope built a fire, and boiled coffee and eggs.

Paradise was such a delightful place to camp in that they decided to stay for another night, for everyone wanted to explore the holly forest, and Rose was more delightful than ever, not to speak of Sarah Wise, who might have been an old wife in a fairy tale, with her grey hair over her shoulders covered with a green wood-cutter's hat, her brown wrinkled face, and her head full of wise sayings and forest lore.

There were whinberries, too, growing in all their purple beauty on the moorland, and whinberries and cream eaten under the green roof of a forest is a feast fit for queens.

They tore themselves away the third day and wended their way across the wild and lovely moorland that leads to Picket Post, from whose height the distant Forest looks like a dim, blue range of hills.

Then they slipped down into the valley and came to the Rufus Stone, where the Red King fell nearly a thousand years ago—long before the gipsies who haunt the spot with souvenirs had stirred in their forest tents.

It was the greatest fun taking "the luck of the road," for one never knew what the next meal would be, and often if they left the highway their luncheon consisted of nothing but brown bread and the early blackberries they found amongst the furze.

They had little meat, though occasionally they swung an iron kettle over a gipsy fire after a long tramp, and Penelope and Wendy made an Irish stew for supper, and every one was expected to forage for the pot. Jill,

Pandora, and Rory trespassed for mushrooms, and Eve provided the flavouring of wild herbs; Nancy and her sisters brought carrots and onions from a cottage garden, and Gladys gave advice and Cassandra wrote a poem in praise of the dish when it was cooked. They lived mostly on bread and butter, fruit, milk and eggs, and before a week was over they were all as brown as real gipsies, and the dresses of the younger travellers were picturesquely ragged and faded. Every one enjoyed every minute of the holiday, and even Gladys owned to herself that she had never had such jolly times at Hastings, even with bands and piers, and niggers to amuse her.

It must be confessed that if Pandora, Jill, and Rory could dodge Gladys and the others, and go on an exploring expedition of their own, they did so; for though Nancy and her sisters were tolerated, Gladys was looked upon as a nuisance to avoid, if possible.

"I thought a school at Idle Pines was *your* idea, as well as mine," said Wendy one day to Pandora.

"Well, it was——"

"Then why don't you show more interest in it?"

"Wendy! I *do*." Pandora was indignant.

"By being rude to the pupils? I can't say you set a very good example in manners, and how can you expect Gladys to improve and take an interest in the things you like, when you avoid her and hurt her feelings by ignoring her?"

Pandora went scarlet. She had been so anxious that all the girls should have a good time at Idle Pines and that it should be a success, and if Gladys wasn't enjoying herself she would probably write home to her father and he would take her away and say ill-natured things about the school. Besides, it wounded Pan in a very tender part to be accused of bad manners.

"But, Wendy; she spoils things."

"So you leave her on my hands—how nice of you,

dear!" and Pan felt horribly penitent, for after all it was Wendy's holiday, too.

After that, Gladys was invited to join the others, and was so flattered that she refrained from calling their amusements "kiddish" and frankly proceeded to enjoy herself.

Notes for the new Doomsday Book were made by the whole party; Eve becoming immensely enthusiastic about the birds of the Forest, and getting up early every morning with Nancy and the younger ones to explore their wildest haunts.

Cassandra collected folk-lore and forest legends, and Jill, Pandora and Rory hunted for wild-flowers, and with the help of a book on the subject, pressed and named them. Wendy drew beautiful maps of the Forest byways, with their local names and landmarks, and Penelope painted charming pictures of famous trees, churches, and cottages.

Gladys, who had a passion for tombstones, insisted upon collecting epitaphs from the churchyards they passed, and to Wendy's astonishment actually began to ask intelligent questions about the foresters and forest laws of long ago.

But it was those adventurers, Jill, Pandora and Rory, now known as the "Inseparables," who provided the most interesting item for the pages of the new Doomsday Book.

They were camping on the outskirts of a Forest village while Penelope finished some sketches; and, exploring as usual, the three girls came across a ruined wall.

There was an old man nearby cutting bracken, and Jill approached him politely.

"Please, can you tell us if this is an *old* wall?

"Ay, he's old right enough, missy—older than you and older than me, too, and I was a babby the year th' old Queen Victoria came to the throne.

"I say, how wonderful! But is it truly awfully old? I mean hundreds of years?

"That's right, missy; he was part of the old manor-house—my old father watched it burn to the ground the night the Big Oak fell in 1813."

"Who lived in it?" demanded Rory.

"'Twas the old home of the Mortimers, missy—all dead and gone out of the Forest now, they be—and the home all burnt to ashes; and they never rebuilt him, they didn't. They do say hereabouts that there's a sight of jewellery and old plate belonging to them at the bottom of yonder well, thrown there by the old Madam Mortimer the night they fired the beacon, and brought her false news that Boney had landed and was marching on to burn the Forest.

"She hated the French like poison, she did, and said she'd never tell where she'd hid the silver till Boney was dead; but she died afore Boney and the old house was burnt and all."

"Down the old well! Oh, where is it?" cried the Inseparables.

"Over there, missy; but don't you go, he's a nasty place with snakes and all, and 'tis all fancy talk about the jewels and silver; for many a lad has near twisted his neck down the well and found nothing but sticks and stones."

But no sooner had the ancient forester hobbled away than the three rushed to seek out the well.

It was almost hidden from sight by brambles. Nettles grew many feet high round the old stones, and the accumulation of dead leaves, ivy, and undergrowth certainly looked as though it might be the favourite abode of snakes.

"Ever since I was born I've been dying to find a treasure," said Pandora, looking at the well rapturously.

"And I'm *going* to find one," cried Jill, with determination.

"Meg had a nurse whose sister was bitten by an adder," said Rory, shivering; "she swelled up and went black and died in awful agony."

"Oh, be quiet, and don't quote that little horror!—besides, I don't believe there *are* snakes," said Pandora. "How lucky it is we are staying another day. Let's get up early, Jill, and bring the rope and explore."

"Rather; look here, Rory, we'll clear away all this rubbish to-night, and if there *are* any snakes they'll jolly well bunk. After all, when you are writing an important book about a county, you can't let snakes stop you from making it interesting."

"Oh, look!" cried Rory suddenly; "there are birds' candles!" and she pointed to the tall mulleins, with their torch-like yellow flowers. "Mary Ellen says it's a safe road wherever they burn."

And with absolute faith in her old nurse's wisdom she proceeded to help to tear away the nettles and rubbish from the old well.

CHAPTER 11

THE FAIRY GODFATHER

But, before the morning, Pan's tiresome conscience had whispered to her that Gladys and Nancy and the little girls would also enjoy a treasure-hunt.

Rather nervously she mentioned this to Jill.

"Take Gladys Shaw down a *well*! There, Wendy said you'd get a touch of the sun if you would go without a hat, and now you have, for you must be quite, quite mad to suggest anything so idiotic."

"Well, Wendy says it's rude to go off enjoying ourselves without them, and after all we should think it horrid if *they* heard of a treasure and never said a word about it."

"I suppose we would," said Jill rather crossly; "but it's too bad, and explorers never drag a crowd with them; but I suppose those two kids will shove themselves, too."

"What a nuisance you are, Pan," said Rory, "always worrying about that awful Gladys. Let's tell them what the old man said about snakes—Gladys isn't the sort of person to poke about amongst adders."

But in spite of Rory's terrible description of the snake-haunted old well, Gladys and the others, grown bolder after their travels, accepted the invitation with alacrity, and preparations for an early morning expedition were made at once.

The stout rope always carried in the caravan was the chief necessity, and Jill also carried a candle and matches, and Pandora took a sharp pocket-knife and Rory a piece of white heather for luck.

The morning dew shone like a jewelled veil over the heather, as they slipped away from the camp after first tying up the "angels," for, much as they hated to do so, even Rory acknowledged that canine angels are too noisy to make good explorers. There was nobody about except little black pigs hunting for acorns, for Forest folk are not fond of early rising.

The yellow flames on the mulleins, which Mary Ellen called birds' candles, encouraged Rory onward; and though Gladys wept at the nettle-stings she got while clearing the undergrowth, and Nancy yawned, and said she thought adventures were just as nice *after* breakfast, things went merrily and nobody "swelled and went black" as Meg's nurse's sister did through an adder bite.

"There!" cried Jill at last, "we can climb up by the stones now and look right down the well. Give me a shove, Pan, and I'll go first."

Pushed up by Pan, who immediately followed her with Rory clinging on to her skirts determined to miss nothing, Jill peeped over the crumbling wall of the well and cried, "I say, it's awfully deep and quite dried-up."

"There seems lots of rubbish," said Pan, also peering over, and Rory, arriving with a spring, cried, "I suppose all the jewels and silver are mixed up with it and that's why nobody can find them."

"I say, Pan, I'm going," said Jill. "Throw up the rope, Nancy."

"I shall go too," said Pan. "Now, Rory, you needn't grab the rope like that, *you* can't come till Jill and I have spied out the land."

"Then I *shall*," announced Rory furiously.

"Then *I* can't go," said Jill, dropping the rope; "somebody with brains always has to be left in command of the rest of the expedition while two or three go forward."

Consoled with the idea that the adored Jill had such faith in her wisdom, Rory consented to allow Pan and Jill to venture forth without her.

"And what can *I* do?" grumbled Gladys.

"Oh, be a sport, for goodness' sake," said Pandora, tying one end of the rope round her waist. "Look here, Jill, if we tie the other end of the rope round that enormous tree-trunk, nobody need hold it and we can swarm up again."

The rope was knotted firmly round the convenient trunk of a big oak, and Pan scrambled over the edge of the well and let herself down boldly.

It seemed ages before the rope tightened with a jerk, and a muffled voice cried, "I say, Jill, do come quickly; I've untied the rope, and it's awfully deep and creepy down here."

Jill disappeared over the edge with a farewell wave to Rory, and a command to watch the road for spies.

More ages seemed to pass before they heard anything from the well, and Barbara and Peggy danced with impatience, for they firmly believed the adventurers would return laden with gold and silver.

At last a voice came from the well. "I say, Rory, look out, I'm coming up."

The watchers saw the rope tighten, and heard the scraping of somebody's sandalled toes against the stone walls; then there was a tearing sound, and a sudden thud—the rope knotted so carefully round the tree had passed over a stone as sharp as a flint, which had cut it through like a knife, under the strain of Pan's ascent.

Rory scrambled up the wall of the well in terror. "Oh, Pan, are you killed?"

"Of course not; don't be silly!" Pan's voice sounded rather queer. "I've only broken my ankle or something."

Then Jill's voice cried, "Look out, Rory, I'm going to throw up the end of the broken rope; catch it and knot it to the other end as firmly as you can."

But, alas! Jill was too good a thrower. The rope sped through the air and caught in the topmost branch of a birch tree, so slender that not even Rory, as daring as a monkey when it came to climbing, cared to risk her life to reach it.

The end of the rope dangling over the wall was far too short for Jill to reach, and the sides of the well so damp and slippery, it was impossible to climb up them without something to hold.

The wildest attempts were made by Rory, without success, to reach the prisoners, and Nancy's suggestion that they should go to a farm not far away for help was scorned by Jill, for it didn't suit her plans to have the forest people know about their search.

"There's a car coming!" cried Peggy suddenly.

"There's a car coming!" shouted Rory down the well. "Oh, Jill, *do* let's ask them to help."

"Very well," called out Jill; "but don't ask *any one*. Wait till somebody really nice comes along."

But as a grey car came sliding round the turn, Barbara and Peggy flung themselves in the road before it.

Rory looked anxiously at the occupant of the car to see if he were "really nice."

"I say, what's up?"

"Oh, please, will you help us? Pandora and Jill are down the well; you see, the rope broke, and we can't get them up again," Rory cried.

"Down the *well*!" then, glancing at the ruined wall and the old well, the nice man murmured, "Well, I'm jiggered!" and Gladys lost all interest in him as a romantic knight.

He jumped out of the car and surveyed Rory. "What on earth are Pandora and Jill doing down the well?"

"You shouldn't ask," said Rory with dignity; "they're down the well because they *like* wells."

"Oh, do they? Well, it seems to be a fashionable amusement in the Forest, for as a matter of fact I got up early on purpose to go down this particular well myself, that's why I brought *this*," and the knight calmly took a thick rope from under the seat of the car.

The row of distressed damsels didn't believe this, but, thankful for the miraculous appearance of a new rope, they led the rescuer to the spot.

With the greatest care he knotted the rope round the oak, then, leaning over the well, he encouraged the injured Pandora to climb, grasping her firmly, and lifting her over directly he could reach her. Looking rather pale and shaky, she collapsed on to the heather, and Jill climbed up the rope like a monkey.

The knight examined Pandora's swollen ankle and said, "I say, that hurts, doesn't it; plucky of you to stick to the rope like that."

The nice man bandaged the ankle carefully then surveyed the heroines whimsically and said, "Pleasant places, damp wells. I suppose you make a study of them?"

"Of course we don't," said Jill, blushing, and thinking it only polite to explain after all his kindness, she continued, "You see, we heard there was a treasure down there, so we went to see."

"Is it rude to ask if you found it?"

"No, we didn't," said Jill, frowning at Pandora, who had opened her mouth to speak, and the nice man said gloomily:

"That's too bad; for, you see, it's *my* treasure, and I rather hoped to find it, too."

"*Your* treasure!" the adventurers gasped.

"Yes; you see, it was my great-grandmother who threw the treasure down the well so that Bonaparte shouldn't get it—I expect the poor old dear imagined that he would cross over from France on purpose to grab her teaspoons!—at least that's the tale, and the old well is all that's left of the house my family lived in for hundreds of years; but when it was burnt they were too poor to rebuild it, and they wandered from the Forest and went abroad. Ever since I was a kiddy I've made up my mind that I'd build a house round the old well again, and hunt for great-grandmother's silver, and now I've arrived to find the well full of brave girls who don't mind snakes and toads and broken ropes in the least."

"But is your name really and truly Mortimer?" asked Jill excitedly, and she glanced at Pandora.

"Rather. Look here, you can't walk to wherever you live with an ankle like that—jump into the car, all of you, and we'll all go and have breakfast at the farm round the corner."

"But first we *must* tell you something," said Pan; "you see, we didn't *find* anything, but we saw something, didn't we, Jill? It was awfully dim and ghostly down there, so we lit a candle and found that part of the wall had been bricked up with *much* newer looking stones than the rest."

Mr. Mortimer at once became as keen as mustard and cried, "What observant little bricks you are; I always believed in the old treasure;" then, glancing at Pan's white face again, he said, "We'll go and have breakfast first, though, and then come back and explore."

The whole party got into the car, and breakfast at the farm was a delightful affair, consisting of hot coffee, hot scones and eggs, eaten under the plum-trees in the orchard, gold and purple with ripening fruit.

Mr. Mortimer was the jolliest person, and before breakfast was over he knew all about Idle Pines, Wendy, the angels, Aunt Sally and Mary Ellen, the Indigestion

School and Moti, and the finding and adoption of Bluebell and the new Doomsday Book.

"What a splendid idea!" he exclaimed. "I'd like to contribute, but all I know about Hampshire is that everything in it is called 'he' but a tom-cat, and he's called 'she,' though for the life of me I can't tell why."

Suddenly Pandora, who had become paler and paler, owned that her foot "throbbed dreadfully," and Mr. Mortimer said she must be taken to the caravan and he would wait to explore the well until the pain was better.

But disappointment awaited them. Wendy, rather bewildered by the sudden appearance of a visitor, a white-faced Pan, and a torrent of news about wells and treasures, broke it to them at once that the postman had just brought a letter to "Tree Tops" saying that the owner of the caravan wanted it as soon as they could bring it home.

It was not a bit of good for Rory to weep, Pandora and Jill to look reproachful, and the chorus to lament— they must break camp immediately.

It was rather a doleful party that started on their homeward way, and Pan had to be in the caravan and nurse her ankle, which was not so exciting as exploring wells, and they were madly curious about the result of their discovery.

They had not long to wait, for about a week after they reached home a fat letter came to Idle Pines, addressed to the "Treasure Seekers," which read as follows:

DEAR EXPLORERS,—Three cheers for old Granny Mortimer! for if she hadn't hidden her best teaspoons from Boney they would have all been melted in the fire when the house burned. The wall *was* bricked up, you clever children, and the country bumpkins who have hunted for the treasure for the last hundred years were too blind to see it. Inside the wall we found a chest

stuffed full of the quaintest old spoons, dishes, and tan-
kards, and some old-fashioned jewels that will look
charming on my wife when I get one and a house to put
her in. I'm going back to China for a year, but when
I come back I shall ask your advice about it all.

"I've been thinking a lot about Bluebell. It's nice
for her to have thirty-four fairy godmothers, but what
a sell it is you never hear of fairy *godfathers* in fairy
tales—nice old chaps they would be in spectacles and
blue cloaks, and lots of original ideas about christening
gifts. I'm frightfully keen on being a fairy godfather,
so do let me begin with Bluebell. I'm sorry we've run
out of magic cloaks, fairy wands, and wishing-caps, but
please give her the enclosed most magical gift with my
love.

"Take it to the Bank and give it to the manager there
who is really a magician in disguise, and he will make
it grow every year.

"Good-bye. Love to yourselves, my goddaughter, the
angels.

"Your affectionate and grateful friend,
"ROGER MORTIMER."

Inside the letter was the most magical piece of paper
—a cheque for a hundred pounds for the school baby!

CHAPTER 12

THE TWELVE DANCING PRINCESSES

No sooner was the excitement about the discovery in the well over than there was another surprise for Bluebell, just after the girls had returned from the holidays.

Wendy was summoned from the open-air schoolroom one September afternoon by Phœbe to see "a young person" in the Library.

The young person was a thin girl, neatly dressed in black, very pale and frightened-looking.

"If you please, Miss, I've come about the little girl."

"The little girl——" Wendy looked puzzled; for the "young person" hardly looked like the relative of a possible new pupil.

"Yes, Miss, the baby that was found in the wood last May."

Wendy looked grave at once.

"Do you mean you know something about that poor deserted mite?"

The girl looked terrified and replied, "Yes, Miss, she's my sister's little one."

"And how on earth was she left alone in the wood, and why have you not claimed her before?"

"It was this way, Miss; my sister was married three years ago to a young gentleman who was a clerk in Westchurch. He died of pneumonia a year this Michaelmas, and left my poor sister with the baby only a few weeks old. He hadn't got a relation in the world, and there wasn't a penny left when he was buried and all, and Alice she was in a poor way, though she never said much at the time. She did a little dressmaking, but she was poorly herself, and at last I got a letter from her landlady saying she was took bad and I was to come at once.

"I do a bit of dressmaking myself up at Sandstone, Miss, and it was a trouble to leave my work at all; but I went right off and found Alice had just passed away, and the poor little girl was alone in the world except for me—me as found it a job to keep myself, Miss. The landlady was a cruel hard woman, and took every penny I had, and even stripped the poor baby except for a little shirt, for she said the clothes belonged to her—I had nothing to put round her except an old green shawl of Alice's. I had to walk all the way from Westchurch, except when a cart gave me a lift."

"But how did you get into the Glen? It is not on the road to Sandstone."

"I lost my way, Miss, and thought it a short cut; so I put the baby down among the flowers while I looked for the path, and the young ladies came and took her away."

"But why did you *let* them do such a thing?"

The girl began to cry. "I don't know, Miss; it came upon me all at once that it was all for the best like—I could see they were young ladies; and I hadn't got a place to put the little one myself and no time to look after her. I found out it was a school they'd taken her to, and the next day I walked over again and saw the bills out, and heard that she was up here in a grand nursery with the best of everything. So I just kept quiet, Miss, though I see now that I didn't ought to have done it."

"And why have you come back now?"

"It was my young man who made me, Miss. We're going to be married next month and going out to Canada, and I told him last night about poor Alice and what

I done with the baby, and he said it wasn't right, and I must come and tell you at once."

"And what do you propose to do?"

"My young man's willing to take her, Miss—not that she'd have what she's been used to here, and we must travel pretty rough—but we're both anxious to do our duty like."

"But do you *want* her?" Wendy turned cold at the thought of an unloved Bluebell journeying as steerage baby to Canada.

The girl hesitated. "Well, Miss, we'll have a struggle, and a baby's a tie, but she must take her chance and we'll do our best."

"Please sit down for a minute." Wendy went straight to the girls and told them that Bluebell was "found."

Every one of the thirty-four fairy godmothers rose in indignation.

"Wendy! you *won't* let her go?"

"How can I help it if they claim her?"

"But they don't *want* her. Don't let her see her, for goodness' sake!" cried Jill.

Wendy looked upset. "I agree with you all that Bluebell is better here, and I will go and talk to her aunt again."

Wendy had a long and serious talk with the pale girl, and told her to bring her young man the next day to see her and talk over the matter. He came, and owned he would be glad if the ladies would adopt the child and give her advantages she could never have from him.

So the whole matter was settled with the help of Mr. Hay, although he didn't approve of Idle Pines adopting a child at all. Bluebell was to become the school baby for ever, and to be provided for by the girls until she could provide for herself, and the fairy godfather's christening gift was to be allowed to grow into a nice little golden nest egg.

"What's her real name?" everybody had demanded at once, and learnt it was "Joy," because poor Alice had said she was such a loving, happy baby.

"Joy isn't so nice as Heart's Delight," said Jill.

"And we shall always call her Bluebell, because you know perfectly well, Wendy, that *They* led the cruel aunt out of her path and gave the baby to *us*," cried Rory.

As soon as Bluebell was really made one of Wendy's children, Laurette called a meeting to discuss ideas about the way to "Brighten Village Life," and Wendy was asked to take the chair.

There were all sorts of ideas—some good and some bad; but in the end it was agreed that Pandora's suggestion was the best, because a great many other ideas could be worked into it, too, if Cassandra were clever.

It was this—that the villagers, young and old, should form a guild to be called "The Forest Guild of Singers and Players," and act plays and little operas, and give pageants and tableaux of incidents in the history of the Forest and the Wessex coast to all the villages around.

"It's an excellent suggestion," said Wendy. "Pandora, you really must not rival me in Ideas like this!

"I suggest that the plays should be sometimes Shakespeare's and sometimes old Elizabethan masques. It would be interesting if they tried to write little plays themselves, too—fairy tale stories that the village children ought to know. I mean, every one should contribute a part, even if it's only one line, which will give them an interest in the play, as well as the pride of authorship. Suppose we tell Miss Caird that they can come up here once a week and we will teach them folk-dancing."

"And we can help them with the dresses; they ought to make everything themselves," said Mary Leslie.

"We could dance in the school-room now it's getting cold," said Wendy; "and use the hall for making properties."

This seemed a jolly way of spending the winter eve-
nings, and then Wendy had another idea. "Why don't
you show the Singers and Players what we mean by
getting up a play yourselves?" she said. "There's still
time enough to have it out of doors, and if you choose
something with plenty of character you can carry out
my idea of joint authorship," and this suggestion was
adopted on the spot.

Cassandra retired to the Sanctuary to write the essay,
and Pandora and Rory made her hot scones and tea *much*
stronger than Mary Ellen allowed, to stimulate her brain.

Everybody agreed that it was a "cookpiece," which
was a word the school delighted to use ever since Nancy
translated "*chef d'œuvre*" in that way for Madame.

Wendy marched them all off to see Miss Caird, and
they sat under her great mulberry tree on the lawn
while Cassandra rather shyly read her masterpiece.

The old lady was charmed, and ordered her staid old
butler to bring out lemonade, ripe plums, and cakes for
the whole party while they talked over the idea.

"To tell the truth I hoped you'd offer to teach the
young people all those charming dances, games, and
songs," she said, with a chuckle. "And quite right,
too; I've no patience with all the folk, rich and poor,
not mixing together in country amusements. You'll
find there's a deal of talent in the village once we can
get it into their heads we're not patronising 'em, poor
dears!

"Now what about the Gift. I've got an idea in my
own old head, and it's this—how would you like me to
build a little out-door theatre in the grounds of Idle
Pines?—something simple—and you could give little
plays to the village folk and for charities, and lend it to
my lads and lasses sometimes when they're clever enough
to have plays of their own."

There was a perfect storm of applause, for nobody

could think of anything more delightful than a real school theatre of their very own.

"We must get William Tanner, that young builder, to join the Singers and Players," said Miss Caird, "and Bill Thoms, the carpenter; then they'll take an interest in the theatre, and it will be much nicer to have it built by the villagers. Now, Miss Wendell—you're an artist, so go home at once and draw me a simple design."

"No; Laurette, Penelope, or Isobel must do that," said Wendy, looking at the school artists. "Now, thank Miss Caird, all of you, and come home to bed at once."

Another meeting was called to decide on a small play to be got up immediately to encourage the would-be Singers and Players—not a very easy task, because Wendy thought a fairy play would be better to begin with, and so few fairy tales had the number of characters they needed.

"I know," cried Rory, turning over a tattered copy of *Grimms'*, "let's have the Twelve Dancing Princesses. There are twelve princes, twelve princesses, the king, the soldier, that's twenty-six, and we could put in a queen and some waiting-maids."

"We'll write the play and then draw for the parts. What do you all say to the Twelve Dancing Princesses, —it seems a good idea."

Every one agreed it was, but when Laurette ordered each girl to draw for the part she was supposed to write, there was a weeping and wailing among the ordinaries.

"It's worse than Miss Dillon's old intelligence tests," groaned Nancy.

"It won't be hard," said Laurette, "for the parts must be short, just a few lines for every one. We must make it more of a spectacle than anything, as there is so little time to learn parts."

Laurette and Cassandra made themselves responsible for the argument of the play, and Cassandra was to open it with the king's proclamation that he would give the hand of one of the twelve princesses to any one who could discover where and how they danced their shoes into holes every night. Penelope was to play and write the queen's part, and the rest of the company were to fit in the parts that followed the opening speech.

In spite of many ups and downs, the preparations for the play went merrily, and there was lots of fun at rehearsals.

With the help of Mary Ellen, they made their dresses with very little expense.

The play was given on a brilliantly sunny October afternoon on the edge of the lake, the audience sitting on the sloping lawn above.

The princesses' sleeping apartment was represented by silken curtains swinging between a group of trees above an old faded Persian carpet, and no sooner did twelve silver chimes ring out than twelve tiny village children, dressed as water-sprites, rose from rushes at the edge of the lake and led the princesses, dancing, across the tiny bridge to the enchanted island. On its shores the princes met them, and under the golden and silver balls swinging in the pine-trees, to represent the lights in the enchanted palace, princes and princesses danced upon the island until the delighted audience simply roared with applause.

Old Miss Caird was delighted with everything, and after tea made a little speech, telling everybody about her plan of an outdoor theatre, and how she hoped that very soon the whole village would be taking part in a play as delightful as the one they had all so much enjoyed that afternoon.

Used to obeying the village fairy godmother, sheepish youths and shy girls were induced to give their names to Wendy, and promised to come up to Idle Pines for an hour twice a week.

William Tanner and Bill Thoms were induced to take an interest in the building of the theatre, and marched off by Miss Caird to Wendy to give their ideas about a site.

Before the sunny October day was over, the "Forest Guild of Singers and Players" was established.

CHAPTER 13

PENELOPE'S WASHERWOMEN

ON Christmas Eve, Pandora, Jill and Rory begged Wendy to let them go for a tramp in the Forest, to gather holly for the house, and she consented on condition that they came home early and did not wander too far away from the beaten track. She would have preferred one of the elder girls to go with them, but Penelope had one of her "cooking crazes," as Jane called it, and Cassandra was busy with Christmas mysteries.

It was a glorious frosty morning and they started off in the highest spirits, each carrying a smoking hot potato baked in its jacket, as well as apples and sandwiches.

Before they had gone many miles they left the forest road and plunged into a rough track through pine-woods.

"We'll show you the King's Council Chamber," promised Rory. "Pan and I call this wood that—the old King is the darlingest pine-tree, and he's got twenty-four courtiers."

They emerged suddenly into a wide clearing, where a ring of fine old pines surrounded an immense tree, covered with cones as big as babies' heads. They lay fallen among the scented pine-needles, too, and Rory called them the King's teasures and began to pick them up to burn with the Christmas log.

The wood was absolutely still—not a sound but the gentle falling of the tawny-coloured cones from the King's crown on to the dry pine needles.

"What a thrilling place," cried Jill; "it looks as though Red Indians might have wigwams somewhere about.

Let's have lunch here; my potato's getting cold and my sandwiches are getting hot; besides, I'm frightfully hungry."

Perfectly willing to linger, Pandora and Rory sat down on the pine-needles and refreshed themselves with warm potatoes.

Then Jill announced calmly, "It *is* a thrilling place, as I said before, but I believe it's haunted."

Pandora said, "Don't be an ass," and Rory wailed, "You're just trying to frighten me, Jill."

"No, I'm not. Really and truly it is. I've ears like cats', you know, and I've heard the queerest rustlings behind the trees for ages, and now just listen. Can't you hear horses' hoofs? Not on the road, but thudding on the turf?"

"I can," admitted Pandora, "but lots of people ride all over the Forest."

"But this sounds like exciting sort of hoofs," went on Jill. "I say, Pan, it might be brigands, and as you and I are rather beautiful, you know, we'd better hide,"—and just to tease Rory, Jill got up and ran, followed by the other two.

Behind the King and his courtiers there was a bank of furze, hollowed out in one place as a thorny shelter for cattle.

"Let's creep in here till the brigand has passed," cried Jill, and Pan—also a tease—and the terrified Rory squeezed into the hollow beside her.

No sooner were they inside than hoofs came thundering nearer and nearer, and, to their utter amazement, a white horse suddenly appeared galloping towards them, ridden by a desperate-looking man in riding breeches, with several pistols sticking in his belt, and thrown across the saddle before him was a *girl*, screaming loudly!

Rory wanted to scream, too, but Jill silenced her so fiercely that, with an effort, she refrained.

To their horror, the man dismounted, tied his horse to a tree, then, swinging the terrified girl over his shoulder as though she had been a bag of flour, he carried her to King Pine.

Here the girl fell on her knees and seemed to be entreating the man for mercy. She had beautiful dark eyes, and her long black hair hung down below her waist. Her flimsy dress and thin, dainty slippers made one suppose that she had been ruthlessly kidnapped from some comfortable fireside.

"He's going to murder her!" murmured Pan tragically; "oh, Jill, what shall we do?"

"Wait," said Jill. She was white and trembling, for this lovely fairy forest seemed suddenly to have turned into a black and sinister place.

Then the man drew out a pistol and held it to the girl's head, and they all shut their eyes; but a fresh scream made them look again to see the girl being gagged and firmly bound to the tree with cords. Then the man mounted his horse and rode away furiously.

"Now's our time!" gasped Jill. "We must set her free before that brute comes back, even if he does murder us for doing it," and she flew out, followed by Pan and Rory, and dashed up to the big tree, where the gagged victim was rolling her eyes in an alarming way.

She rolled them still more when she saw the three girls, and began to make the wildest signs.

"Oh, never mind," comforted Pandora; "we'll get you out of this in a jiffy. What an *awful* brute!" and Jill whispered, "Keep still. Oh, if *only* we had had knives. Rory, you untie the lower knots while I——"

Then such exciting things began to happen that even Jill collapsed on to the pine needles weakly and Rory could refrain from screaming no longer.

A splendid person on a dark horse dashed through the pines, and then, from all directions, came the queerest crowd—more the sort of people one meets in dreams than in a quiet English forest. Some looked remarkably like Red Indians, some wore daggers and a great many pistols, and a stout little man in a fur overcoat stood behind a *camera* on thin legs, and danced up and down like a maniac and seemed to be swearing at them.

Then the murderer on the white horse came galloping back and set the gagged girl free, and she at once sat down on the pine-needles beside her rescuers and rolled about in helpless laughter, while the other people talked and shouted all together.

"Oh, you darling, priceless infants!" gasped the girl at last.

"Oh, what *have* we done?" asked Pandora miserably.

"*Done*—spoilt the film, I expect. Mr. Parker looks quite, quite mad——"

"The *film*!" The three girls stared helplessly.

"Yes, you sweet little idots. Didn't you guess we were filming? This place is just right for a Canadian forest scene. Mr. Parker, do stop raving. We can begin again, and I want these infants to have front seats, please, for saving my life so beautifully."

"Front seats!" roared the producer of the film; "tie 'em to the trees and gag 'em, you mean!" and Rory shuddered.

But, after more talk, the hero on the dark horse seemed to make things right, and, to the girls' joy, they were told they could watch the rehearsal if they kept out of the way.

So the next hour was blissfully exciting. The lovely girl was kidnapped, gagged and bound again, and was then rescued by the splendid hero, who carried her away on the dark horse, after wounding several Red Indians and the desperate villain.

To make a perfect ending to the day, the charming actress took them home in her car, stopping on the way at a confectioner's in a forest village, where she bought each of them a gorgeous box of chocolates for "saving her life so splendidly!"

When they arrived home, Penelope and Cassandra lamented loudly that they had not shared the exciting experience; but Wendy said she did not like to think of her lovely forest turning into cinema-land, and Mary Ellen remarked that no wonder "*They*" were never seen nowadays with "such goings on."

But the three girls had enjoyed every moment of the spectacle, and looked forward to giving a thrilling reproduction of the whole scene in the pine-wood when their friends came back to school.

They were all busy the first part of the holidays helping the Forest Players and Singers to get up the old mumming play, St. George and the Dragon, as a surprise for Miss Caird. Then the delighted old lady gave a splendid party, so that Christmas, which Wendy had rather dreaded—the first one her four pupils had ever spent without their beloved father—was a merry one after all.

All the pupils came back early in February, and work began again in earnest; for, although there were no marks or rewards to be gained, the girls looked upon it as a disgrace not to be as keen about their work as play, and even the "ordinaries," were ashamed of shirking and knew a great deal more about Timbuctoo and the number of a Kaffir's legs than when they first came to Idle Pines.

Cassandra, who was usually first in classical subjects, had for months nursed a secret ambition to gain the scholarship to be given in memory of her father; but she feared it would not be fair for the honour to remain in the family.

She came to Wendy one day and broached the subject nervously.

"I say, Wendy, I'm awfully keen on getting that scholarship."

"Well, my dear child, why shouldn't you?"

"Wouldn't it seem grabby?"

"What nonsense; you are a pupil of the school and have no privileges because you belong to the house, so why should you not have the same advantages as the rest? You must work, though—Laurette is pretty good; her Latin prose was really excellent this week."

"I know; but I *can* work, you know, Wendy."

"Well, go ahead, dear, and nobody will be better pleased than your old Wendy if you win."

Cassandra set to work at once, for Laurette was older and quite a formidable rival, especially in Latin; but before a week had passed something happened to change Cassandra's mind.

She was rather chummy with Isobel Clifton, a shy, clever girl with little self-confidence and a genius for effacing herself.

Isobel came back to school rather quieter than usual, and with a habit of going off by herself which rather puzzled Cassandra.

One wet Saturday afternoon, when everybody else had gone for a tramp on the moor with the indomitable Dorothy, Cassandra found Isobel in the music-room poring over exercise-books and decidedly red about the eyes.

Pretending not to notice, Cassandra, who had stayed at home "to peg away at Latin," instantly felt a desire to do something for the woe-begone Isobel, and said carelessly, "I say, Isobel, what idiots we were not to go for the tramp; let's put on our boots and raincoats and follow them."

"I'm sorry, but I really can't, Cassandra."

"Why not?"

"Because I'm such an ignorant duffer. I've made up

my mind to give up nearly all my rec. to study this term; I'll simply *have* to do it."

"Don't be absurd; you're all right. Why, Wendy only said yesterday you were steady in everything and quite brilliant in maths."

"Yes; but I'm miles behind you and Laurette in classics; and—you'll think it a frightful cheek, I know, Cassandra, but I might as well tell you I'm frightfully keen on winning the scholarship."

Cassandra went scarlet. She had never thought of Isobel as a rival, and it was really absurd of her to compete with Laurette and herself.

"You *do* think it cheek, I see, but I'm going to peg away to get through if I can, because if I don't it means leaving Idle Pines in May."

"*Leave*—but why?"

"Dad's had frightful losses lately, and he says if the boys are to go to Harrow—and they *must*, because Dad and all my uncles went there—the girls will have to be content with lessons in languages and music at home, and it's not the same, of course. I'm going to work for the scholarship with all my wits, though how I'm going to beat *you* goodness knows, and I wouldn't try, only I know you'll stay at Idle Pines whether you gain a scholarship or not."

"Just my luck!" thought Cassandra despondently, and it was on the tip of her tongue to say, "But I want it frightfully too, because it's given in my father's name," when Isobel added, "You see, it's so lovely at Idle Pines, and at home—I've got a stepmother."

A stepmother instead of Wendy! Cassandra, with the quick sympathy of most imaginative people, made up her mind in an instant and said, "Oh, how horrid for you. I say, Isobel, look here, I'll help you if you like; I'd love to, and it's much easier than pegging away alone."

"But what about you?"

"I'm not trying; I don't believe it would be fair. You see, father was such a wonderful classical scholar and he helped me such heaps."

Unsuspicious, and with her worst rival removed and offering to coach her, Isobel brightened up wonderfully, and accepted Cassandra's offer with such gratitude that the latter found it easier to bear her very real disappointment.

The result of this conversation was that Cassandra and Isobel spent more time together than ever, and Isobel's work improved every week and Cassandra's was so uninspired that Wendy summoned her to the sanctum.

"Cassandra, didn't you mean what you said to me about the scholarship; surely you don't think you are so far ahead of the others that there is no need to work?"

"Of course not, Wendy; but I've changed my mind; I'd rather not try for the scholarship after all."

"May I ask why?"

"I'd rather not—that's all, Wendy," and Cassandra, always the most reserved of the four girls, turned away in silence, leaving Wendy puzzled and disappointed.

But if she was disappointed in Cassandra, she was growing proud of Penelope.

Penelope, the pensive, the dreamy and forgetful maiden, was becoming such an efficient housewife, that Wendy often said that in a few years she would be able to go on the school staff as mistress of domestic science, and it was not long before Penelope proved she would be capable of undertaking such a task.

One day, when the March wind was singing over the gorse, and the last crocuses stood up in the flower-beds like golden lighted tapers, one of those domestic crisis that will happen in even the best managed houses arose at Idle Pines.

Mary Ellen said it was Aunt Sally's fault, because she cut down the rowan-tree near the kitchen door, just because it shaded the plum-tree on the wall too much; and of course without a rowan-tree as a protection *They* get into the house and begin their tormenting tricks. The first thing the creatures did was to put whitlows on Mary Ellen's two thumbs. They then gave Jane a "bad leg," and Phœbe's mother a heart attack, so that she had to go off and nurse her at a moment's notice. They then caused Tilly to get into one of her tantrums, and put it into the head of Mrs. Cobb, the Idle Pines' laundress, to send a note saying she could not "oblige" by doing the school washing for another fortnight on account of her married daughter being laid up.

Unfortunately, in a coast village everybody was busy spring-cleaning in readiness for Easter visitors, nobody else was willing to oblige either, and the washing lay in the laundry in alarming quantities, with nobody to do it, as the younger maids were too busy already with Phœbe away and Mary Ellen and Jane both invalids.

It was then that Penelope woke up and became practical in an astonishing way, and actually called a meeting which she addressed herself.

It lasted an hour, and at the end of it Penelope marched into the sanctum and made a request to Wendy.

"Wendy, if we work all rec. time to-morrow and the next day, and on Saturday afternoon, please can we have a whole holiday to-morrow?"

"A *whole* holiday! But my dear child, why?"

"Because we want to do something."

"But what is it?"

"Please don't ask; it's a secret. But we won't go out of bounds, and it's something useful *and* ornamental, and something that will benefit the school and every one in it."

Wendy thought for a moment; she believed in trusting

the girls and not being too insistent about knowing all their doings.

"Very well; but I shall expect you to make up for all lost time, remember."

"Of course we will; thanks awfully, Wendy," and Penelope marched away to report her success.

At six o'clock next morning a strange procession left Idle Pines. Penelope drove the donkey-cart round to the laundry, and was received by thirty-three girls, their sleeves also rolled up in a workmanlike manner. The cart was loaded with several overflowing clothes baskets, a large copper cauldron, a big packet of soap, several kettles and a huge covered basket.

Then Penelope led the donkey and the whole party went through the gates of Idle Pines, and took the sandy path which led to the gurgling tawny-coloured stream that sang all the way through the Glen to the sea.

When they reached the plank bridge which crossed the stream to the gorse-covered cliffs, the procession came to a halt.

Eve's patrol picked up sticks at lightning speed and made a huge fire, over which the copper cauldron was supported by bricks and stones. Cassandra's seven filled it with kettles and cans of water from the stream, while Isobel's sorted out the piles of clothes in the baskets, and Mary Leslie found a dry, turfy spot looking over the sea, where she laid a tablecloth and set her protégées to spread honey on the huge pile of bread she cut.

Penelope, with a crowd of attendants, then proceeded to the banks of the stream, and kneeling on the stepping-stones they began to wash the clothes in the clear soft water.

By the time Mary had the kettles boiling for breakfast, the big cauldron contained its first boiling of white clothes, and the washerwomen were able to rest from their labours and refresh themselves with large quantities of bread and honey.

Some of the girls washed the clothes for the cauldron, others rinsed the clean ones in the stream, and the rest wrung them out and carried them up the cliff and spread them out on the gorse-bushes.

Pandora had the brilliant idea of damming a small part of the stream, and squeezing the blue-bag into it for the final rinsing, an idea the juniors thoroughly enjoyed carrying out, though it was a pity that Jill and Rory in their artistic efforts to make this natural blue-tub look like a "darling little Italian lake," made it so blue that a great many clothes had to be re-boiled.

By noon everything was finished and the gorse-bushes were patched with white instead of gold.

At two o'clock the procession started homewards, with the donkey—who had escaped three times and eaten half Aunt Sally's nightgown off a furze-bush—gaily decorated with daisy chains, and the wagon loaded with sweet, gorse-scented clean clothes.

Wendy and the teaching staff, meekly working in the garden under the vigilant eye of the slave-driving Aunt Sally, watched the procession enter the drive, and Miss Dillon promptly photographed it. Dorothy gave a cheer and Wendy looked as a proud mother of an industrious family would.

The clothes were carried into the laundry, and the rest of the afternoon spent in folding, sprinkling the clothes, and mangling and ironing; and at five o'clock the washer-women rather wished a magic feast would appear.

And so it did. Mary Ellen, smiling with pride, came and marched them off to the big dining-room, where a magnificent tea, presided over by Wendy, of scrambled eggs on toast, hot scones and jam awaited them.

"Sit down, all of you," she ordered, "and rest your backs and eat a hunter's tea. I never thought I should ever have thirty-four nice charladies to "oblige" me at once. You are all splendid children and I am really proud of you."

"And Jill and I have washed every *bit* of colour out of Madame's green dressing jacket," whispered Rory to Mary Ellen. "So if it was that which was making *Them* so horrid we shall be all right now."

"Whist, with your green dressing-jackets!" cried Mary Ellen. "It's me that's been and got rid of the creatures, for I've made a pudding in an egg-shell and took no notice of that Jane's sarcastic remarks, and you'll see, lovey, *They* won't bide in a house mean enough to make a pudding as small as that!"

Whether it was the disappearance of the green from Madame's most cherished dressing-jacket, or the size of Mary Ellen's pudding, nobody knows; but certainly luck returned to Idle Pines. Mary Ellen lost her whitlows, Tilly recovered her temper, Jane's leg "took a turn for the better," Phœbe returned, and Mrs. Cobb was able to "oblige" the next week after all.

The result of the day's work was that the girls proved they were capable of dealing with an emergency, and Madame Clément said to Wendy that night, "It is the little quiet Penelope who gains the *cordon blen—hein?* "

CHAPTER 14

THAT Gladys Shaw really was not such an awful child as when she came to Idle Pines was proved soon after the great Washing Day. "Poppa" telegraphed to say he was paying his daughter a flying visit one spring day, which caused joy to Gladys and curiosity in the whole school; for every one was anxious to see him. A little to the girls' disappointment, he was a thin, nervous little man, in a white waistcoat, who called Wendy "Ma'am," Miss Dillon and Dorothy "Miss," Madame Clément "Madam-er-selle"—with an absurd little foreign bow —Gladys "my pet," and the rest of the girls "young ladies." He arrived on a half-holiday, and, anxious to give "my pet" a treat, he suggested a jaunt to Bourne-mouth with a few of the other young ladies, to see a film, followed by tea in some place where a band played.

It was then that Gladys showed that she was a worthy pupil of an open-air school.

"Oh, Poppa, don't be stuffy, *please*," she exclaimed. "There's an old man here with wagonettes and nice fat horses; we'll jog along in those and *see* things. We'll go for a picnic in the Forest, and of course you must invite *all* the girls."

Poppa was astounded, and delighted, too.

So he said amiably, "That will be fine, my pet."

Poppa obeyed orders meekly, and the whole school jogged off to the Forest in wagonettes decorated with primroses. They made tea themselves and did full justice to the chocolate cakes, which Gladys's father bought at the hotel, and rewarded Poppa afterwards by taking him scouting in the thick glades; an experience he enjoyed as much as any schoolboy.

Before he left he thanked Wendy enthusiastically for all she had done for "his girl," and anxiously inquired when she would receive Gladys's little sisters, for he seemed very keen on owning a family of open-air girls.

"I expect when Gladys gets home she will simply tear the other kids' velvet dresses from their backs," prophesied Rory.

"And make ' momma ' camp out in a tent instead of staying at a boarding-house at Hastings," said Cassandra.

"Well, you said you would turn her into a nice blue-serge-open-air girl, and you have, you clever Wendy," put in Pandora proudly, for she also had had a hand in the reforming of Gladys.

Spring came early to Idle Pines. The big larch in the Glen, that all through the dull autumn days had stood like a blazing pillar of gold, was now clad in the softest green in all the woodlands, and the pale anemones were spread like a starry heaven beneath the pine-trees round the Sanctuary.

To quote Mary Ellen, "the Spring got into Rory's legs," which made her trying enough to vex a dozen saints; and perhaps that was what was the matter with Jill, too, for she had an adventure before the term was over which might have ended tragically.

Rory adored Jill; and Jill managed Rory wonderfully —better than Mary Ellen and the entire staff did, but all the same she could not resist teasing her sometimes, and she did it by pretending to be a sleep-walker, or somnambulist as she preferred to call it. It was certainly true she *had* walked in her sleep occasionally in her infancy, but it was a habit she had fortunately outgrown, though her love of teasing made her keep this fact from Rory.

Every night poor Rory, however tired, would keep herself awake until Jill seemed to be sleeping too soundly to wander on cliffs, and there was never a night that she did not ask anxiously, "Do you think you will walk to-night, Jill?"

Sometimes the mischief-loving Jill, anxious to keep up her reputation, rose from her bed and, with closed eyes, dressed and wandered about the room, while Rory endured agonies of apprehension; but Jill walked only long enough to tease the watcher, and, returning to bed, pretended to know nothing at all of the occurrence in the morning.

One warm night in early April, Jill lay wakeful and restless, listening to the waves softly kissing the shore, and wishing she could run to the yellow sands and watch them instead of lying wide-awake in a dormitory listening to the snores of the unimaginative Meg Connell.

She slipped out of bed and looked out of the window. The moonlight lay like a pool of silver under the pine-trees, and Jill felt certain that she could hear the first faint trill of a nightingale in the distance. Suppose it were singing in the almond-tree on the enchanted island —how perfectly delicious it would be to creep out into the garden all alone and listen to the nightingale's song. She could see how the golden sallows looked by the margin of the lake in the moonlight, offering their honey-feast to the night moths.

Always ready to act on impulse regardless of consequences, she slipped her rose-coloured dressing-gown over her warm night things and drew on her slippers. Every one seemed to be sleeping soundly, and, without a thought about sleep-walking, and quite unconscious that Rory was watching her anxiously, Jill left the room quietly.

Rory sat up in bed with a horrified gasp—the worst had happened. Jill was walking in her sleep and was making her way to the cliffs, and would probably be drowned if nobody followed her.

Remembering with a shiver all the terrible things she had heard happened to sleep-walkers if they were awakened suddenly, Rory waited for a few moments. Then she stole out of bed, dragged on her dressing-gown and slippers, and made her way to Sparta.

Pandora, dreaming happily, was rudely awakened by feeling a tug at her plaits.

"Hush! don't be an idiot and wake everybody. Something awful has happened—Jill's walking in her sleep, and she's gone to the cliffs to drown herself."

But, in spite of Rory's warning, Pandora's waking cry aroused the whole dormitory, and Eve sat up and said crossly, "What on earth's the matter?"

Julie, awake at once, was ready for excitement as usual and questioned Rory eagerly, but Pauline and Nancy said, unsympathetically, that if Jill walked over the cliffs it was her own fault, and very likely Mary Ellen would prefer her to be drowned to the whole school catching a Cold through going to rescue her.

"Oh, do come—*do* come!" wailed Rory, wringing her hands in despair; and Eve, realising things were serious, jumped out of bed, and, anxious to prove she was capable of managing the whole affair, ordered every one else to be quiet and she would have that tiresome Jill back in bed in a jiffy.

But Pandora was already in her dressing-gown, and there was no time to argue with Rory, so the three set out on their quest, and no sooner had they gone than everybody else jumped out of bed and made a rush for dressing-gowns and slippers; for even the sleepy Pauline couldn't keep quiet while Pandora and Rory hunted for a sleeping Jill in the moonlight.

They stole down the quiet corridors, kindly stopping

at Somnus and Æolus on their way, to wake up the sleepers there and press them to join in the search.

In the meantime, Jill had left the house by the garden door just as the hall clock struck twelve, and made for the enchanted island with a courage that really amazed herself.

Under the pine-trees the bracken fronds were uncurling their tiny green goblin fists, and the pale primroses gleamed like fallen stars.

Jill picked a handful of them and twisted them in her dark hair, and danced in the pool of moonlight like some wild wood-nymph, then she turned round suddenly and her heart gave such a leap into her throat it almost suffocated her, for never had she seen such an amazing and inexplicable sight.

Behind her lay the garden, shadowy and silent, and flitting down its paths in all directions were *girls*—little girls and big girls, all clad in dressing-gowns, mauve, scarlet, pink and blue, looking like bright-coloured night moths fluttering in the moonlight.

What *could* it mean? Surely *everybody* hadn't gone mad in the moonlight and left their beds for a ramble round the garden!

Slipping into the shadows, Jill watched them in astonishment. There, in her straight boyish dressing-gown, was Eve, who seemed to be scolding everybody. Maisie Hill, without her spectacles, short-sightedly fell over a tub of wallflowers, and Pauline, with a pair of woollen gloves on, and a scarf tied over her head, seemed to be remonstrating as usual. Pandora, in a scarlet robe and her mop of hair flying over her shoulders, was restraining Rory, and Rory—when Jill looked at Rory the truth came upon her with a flash. Her elfin face was pale and woebegone, and she was biting the end of one of her plaits, as she always did when in trouble and doubt. She had evidently discovered Jill's disappearance and roused the whole school, and they were dodging round trees and shrubberies so that the sleep-walker should not be awakened suddenly and die with the shock she had threatened.

Jill's first desire was to burst into shrieks of laughter. Oh, what an awful pity she had not thought of this glorious idea on the First of April! Should she keep up the delusion and return to the house, with the whole crowd following her like sleuth-hounds in some thrilling detective story, and go to bed and feign ignorance of everything in the morning, or should she make things more thrilling even than they were already?

A gentle whinny from the paddock near decided her. The evening before she and Pandora and Rory had put their ponies there to be in readiness for some jumping practice during the morning recreation. How glorious it would be to mount Charmion and gallop away to the Forest, and just see if the dressing-gown-brigade would round-up all the ponies of Idle Pines too!

Walking slowly, she went through the iron gate into the paddock and called Charmion softly, and led him into the gate opening into the lane that ran to the Common. Then, to the horror of the watchers in the garden, she suddenly seized Charmion's mane, swung herself up on to his back, and galloped off in the direction of the Forest.

Eve was not in sight at the moment; for, having some idea of guiding Jill back gently, she had slipped round another path.

Pauline said, " *Now* she'll break her neck, and nobody can say it's *our* fault—all catching pneumonia in a damp garden as fast as we can."

Rory, overwrought with anxiety, and driven to despair by Meg's tales of sleep-walkers who had walked into wells and over cliffs, threw herself on the damp ground and wept, and Pandora, gathering up her scarlet robes, said firmly, "I shall follow her on Redskin."

"Then so shall I," cried Rory, starting up.

"No, you won't," Pandora spoke fiercely; "Jill will be killed if you do. Redskin is as quiet as a lamb—you know he is; but if you bring Jackyboy into it, he's such a wild little gipsy he'll spoil everything."

That Jackyboy was wild and unmanageable if excited, Rory could not deny, so she cast herself on the ground again, while Pandora caught Redskin, regardless of the entreaties of the other girls, who felt that things would be getting too thrilling if somebody else galloped off to the Forest on a bare-backed pony in the middle of the night.

It must be confessed that when Pandora mounted the wondering Redskin and rode towards the wide, open Common, her heart beat even louder than her pony's hoofs. All her life she had had only one fear—she was terrified of gipsies. Once, when a very small child, she had run away from Mary Ellen in a temper to the Forest, and been frightened to death by a black-browed gipsy, who carried her off to a tent among the thorn-trees, where a dirty old gipsy woman smoked a pipe and spoke the Romany—a language which sounded to the terrified Pandora as though she were uttering some awful spell or curse.

She had never forgotten this adventure of her childhood, and a plunge at midnight into a Forest, well known to be the haunt of gipsies of all sorts, made her shudder with fear; but such a thought as letting Rory go, or waiting until a search-party could be called to the rescue, never entered her head.

She was devoted to Jill, and Jill was in danger and must be brought home at all costs, or disgrace fall upon Idle Pines; for even Pandora, headstrong and fond of adventure herself, realised it was not *convenable*, as Madame would say, for a pupil of any well-behaved school to wander through a forest unattended in the middle of the night, and Pandora was always over-anxious about Wendy's venture and the well-being of Idle Pines. So on she galloped, straining her eyes in the moonlight for a glimpse of a rose-coloured rider on a white steed.

Meanwhile Jill galloped, too, Charmion enjoying the night ride as much as his mistress; for he had wild Arab blood in his veins and loved adventures.

They soon left the Common behind them and came to the wide, open spaces of the Forest, where the pine-trees stood in the moonlight like tall, dark sentinels helmeted with silver.

"It's a great wild Forest, and I'm *in* it riding, riding in the middle of the night! Oh, how glorious!" sang Jill over and over again, her wild spirits becoming wilder every moment.

Then, suddenly, Charmion stumbled over the roots of an old tree and came crashing to the ground, and Jill was thrown down, down into a darkness deeper than the shadows of any wild Forest.

Pandora, galloping behind on steady little Redskin, was alarmed at that moment by the sudden hooting of an owl, and the quick scamper of a large hare across her path.

"What an idiot I am," she murmured; "as bad as Mary Ellen, and she would say it was horrible luck to have a hare cross my path like that. I wonder if witches really *do* turn into hares at night. I believe they do, but what a row I should get into with Wendy if I said so— Oh, Jill! Jill!"

Her voice rang out in a terrified cry, for no sooner had the hare disappeared than she galloped round a group of pines just in time to see Charmion stumble, and Jill thrown to the ground.

"*Now* she'll wake and have a fit and go out of her mind," she moaned, and, forgetful of the dark pines, with, perhaps, a gipsy lurking behind every one of them, Pandora raced to Jill's rescue.

Before she reached the spot the terrified Charmion had scrambled to his feet and galloped away, but, to her horror, Jill never moved, but lay on her face so still that Pandora trembled. She slipped from Redskin's back and knelt on the ground by the tumbled heap of rose-coloured silk. Redskin, always quiet, stood near, placidly munching the turf.

She gently pushed the hair from Jill's face—it was whiter than the moonlight which lay in a deep pool round them, and her strange stillness made Pandora almost sob with fear.

"Oh, what shall I do? what shall I do?" she whispered. "There's nobody anywhere and I believe she's dying. Oh, Jill, wake up; do, *do*, dear, please."

Jill lay still, and there was not a sound in the Forest except the far cry of an owl and the munching of Redskin near her.

"I must leave her here and tear away home for help," thought the distracted Pandora.

Then, looking at the still figure again, she knew she could not do that, for the ground was damp and cold; gipsies might come, or an adder dart out and bite the unconscious Jill.

Suddenly Pandora had an idea, and she leapt to her feet. One of the favourite amusements of the four girls in the old days was to teach the ponies tricks, and they occasionally gave a grand circus performance in the paddock for the entertainment of the household. Redskin could never be persuaded to jump as well as that wild gipsy Forest pony Jackyboy; but at a word from Pandora he would lie down like a lamb.

Seizing him by the mane, Pandora whispered in his ear and he obediently lay down close to Jill, as a wise camel might to receive his load.

Pandora gently dragged the unconscious Jill on to his broad back, then, holding her firmly, in tender, coaxing tones she told the gentle Redskin to rise, and, turning him towards home, they began their journey.

Away in the garden of Idle Pines there was the greatest excitement after Pandora's departure. Eve returned and scolded violently, and then, realising the situation was too serious for her to manage alone, she marched to the house and roused Wendy with the announcement that Jill had gone riding bareback in the Forest fast asleep and Pandora had kindly followed to wake her up!

Wendy wasted no time in words. Very pale and quiet, she ordered the girls to bed, roused Mary Ellen, and, dressing swiftly, she went to the stable, saddled her own mare, and galloped after the runaways.

Mary Ellen had every girl in bed in a twinkling and gave each one a scolding and a dose of her detestable lozenges. Rory, she carried off to the nursery, tenderly coaxing and comforting the weeping child, who was so sure her precious Pan and Jill would never return.

"Never come back, lovey, that they will. Bad pennies always do; and if I was Miss Wendell I'd shut them in the Tower room for a week, starting a Spring Cold like this; they must be fairy-taken, the wild little hussies!"

She lit a huge fire, boiled hot water and warmed a pile of blankets in readiness for the truants, never letting Rory guess how anxious she felt.

But even Mary Ellen couldn't keep three dormitories of excited girls in bed; and when she had vanished to the nursery, and the senior girls had gone to the hall to listen and wait, they were all up, and had their faces pressed to the windows when Pandora, weary, white-faced, and holding the still figure of Jill on Redskin's back, entered the gates of Idle Pines in the moonlight. Thrilled by this amazing sight, Pandora, always a favourite, at once became the school heroine.

Arriving by a short cut, she had unfortunately missed Wendy; and when the latter, paler than ever, came galloping back, Jill had been carried upstairs, while Dorothy raced away for a doctor and Penelope put the shaking Pandora to bed.

An anxious night passed, but at noon the next day Jill —suffering, the doctor said, from concussion of the brain—opened weary eyes and asked about Charmion, who had been brought home lame but chastened. Assured of his safety, she drank the nourishment Wendy gave her and sank into a quiet sleep. The news was carried downstairs by Mary Ellen, and Rory's woe-begone face became hopeful again and Pandora's heavy eyes shone with relief. Later in the day this hopeful Pandora, always anxious to do her best, and often doing her worst so successfully, was made the happiest girl in the world. She was getting ready to practise in the music-room when she heard one of the girls in the garden below say enthusiastically, "Well, I think it was simply *splendid* of Pandora," and somebody else replied, "Of course it was, but I've said all along that Pandora was the jolliest girl in the school."

With a bound Pandora's thoughts flew to that bleak January day more than a year ago, when she and the others sat on the veranda and planned to turn Idle Pines into a school, and she had said so lightly, "Oh, I shall be the jolliest girl in the school, of course."

To think it had come *true*, and that everybody liked her, and Jill was better and Wendy had little dimples at the corners of her mouth again!

Slipping downstairs she ran into the paddock, where Redskin was placidly munching.

"Angel," said Pandora, rapturously hugging his red nose; "do you know you are a duck, and all through you, your own own missus is really and truly 'the-jolliest-girl-in-the-school!'"

CHAPTER 15

MAY REVELS

JILL, sick and languid, with a head too heavy to raise from her pillow, was inclined to be sorry for herself when she made her confession to Wendy about her imaginary sleep-walking.

"Don't pity yourself, my dearest child," said Wendy, "for self-pity is as demoralising as that very common complaint nowadays called ' an artistic temperament '"—Jill blushed—"which so many people selfishly make the excuse for doing and saying exactly what they wish. Your head is aching terribly, I know, and that should be enough punishment for you; but to show you all that I do not intend you to abuse the liberty that is given to you I intend to be a real old-fashioned school-mistress in this case, and in future the dormitory doors will be locked by Mary Ellen at ten o'clock. I won't want a school full of story-book heroines. I want nice, sensible children, ready to do the right thing at the right moment."

"But Pandora *is* a heroine," protested Jill, feeling horribly disappointed that she was not considered to be one, too; for if she'd gone on a moonlight ramble at the " No Rules " school, Miss Seton would have considered her interesting, she knew, and here was Wendy snubbing her—all the same she adored Wendy and detested the gushing Miss Seton.

"If Pandora hadn't followed me on Redskin, I should have perhaps been trampled upon by the Forest ponies," she continued dolefully.

"Very well, then, Pandora shall be the school heroine,

as you seem so determined to have one, and Cassandra the school blue-stocking."

"And what am I?"

"The black sheep of the school! But you mustn't ' baa ' any more now; go to sleep like a nice little white lamb, and after tea the Heroine and the Blue-stocking, and perhaps ' the-youngest-girl-in-the-school,' shall come to see you."

When the pains in her head grew less Jill began to enjoy her convalescence. The girls brought her all the school news, and Penelope made her delicious jellies and spongecakes.

Even Aunt Sally stumped upstairs in her seven league boots occasionally, and though outwardly seeming to be unsympathetic, there was a twinkle in her eye, and she always brought some unexpected and delightful gift from the garden.

"Still lying here?" she would cry in horror. "Well, I never could stand lackadaisical gels lying in bed with fingers that look as though they'd never touched a weed for a month. Here's a bit of the first apple-blossom for you—they'd have made a couple of nice pies if I'd left 'em on the trees; but if you'd rather have blossom than pies there you are. And for goodness' sake rouse yourself gel, and come and give a hand with thinning out the parsnips."

She put an exquisite spray of apple-blossom close to Jill's nose and stumped away; but Jill loved to see her weather-beaten face and hear her loud voice, for every one had grown fond of Aunt Sally, and if a baronet's daughter who had two bishops for uncles liked to say "gel" and sometimes lapse into the Hampshire dialect, what did it matter to any one?

But Miss Dillon surprised Jill the most. Nobody had ever quite understood Miss Dillon, for, as Pandora said, she could never be described as a "mean old thing," and yet nobody considered her "a perfect darling" either.

She taught excellently, and was always just, although a little sarcastic sometimes. She said little, and there was a belief among the juniors that she was preparing fresh tortures for "poor kids" by writing dry-as-dust text-books in her spare time.

Therefore Jill was astounded when she came in one morning and said rather whimsically, "As you are an invalid, Marguerite—your own fault, of course—I thought perhaps this would amuse you."

She put a slender, green-covered book on the bed and Jill was instantly devoured with curiosity when she read its title, "The Busy Bees of Idle Pines."

She was excited, too, when she opened it, for it was a story of the school; its work, its aims, its failures, the adoption of the school baby and the founding of the Forest Guild of Singers and Players. There was a description of the great Washing Day, too, illustrated by photographs taken by Miss Dillon, and it is so thrilling to see your picture in a *real* book even if nobody knows what your name is. When Pandora and Rory came upstairs they were let into the secret, and before evening the whole school had read the truth about themselves with interest and felt immensely proud of being one of the Idle Pines' Busy Bees. This was much more interesting than text-books and Miss Dillon was looked upon as a person of whom to be proud from that moment.

When Jill, rather white-faced and shaky, was well enough to lie on the sunny veranda, there came a letter from India which gave her great joy.

Moti was coming home again in May—in time to carry Jill off somewhere for the Easter holidays, and afterwards she intended taking a house near Idle Pines for the summer months. She was bringing with her from India three little girls, whose parents very much hoped Miss Wendell would take under her care on their arrival.

"But they'll be *little* girls, and you said you didn't want to have small children, Wendy," objected Cassandra.

"I know I did; but I've had so many letters from people in India since Jill came to us, I am beginning to think it would be an excellent idea to have a lower school almost especially for Anglo-Indian children.

"Some more little girls will be good for Rory—Mary Ellen *will* make a baby of her—and good for Bluebell, too, she is in danger of becoming the school tyrant. We'll build a new wing on the west side of the house, and when it is ready we will ask Mr. Hay to luncheon and show him what a very popular school Idle Pines has become. Poor man, how disappointed he will be!"

Great preparations were being made for the fifth of May, for this day was the school's birthday, the breaking-up, and the occasion of the opening of Miss Caird's gift to Idle Pines of the out-door theatre.

It stood on the old bowling green, a very simple erection, like a small Greek temple. The stage was circular and raised about four feet from the ground, and on each side of it rose a tall, fluted pillar of dark pine-wood, beautifully carved by one of Miss Caird's protégées.

Up these slender pillars Aunt Sally has planted wistaria, purple and white—chosen because it hung its rich and graceful blossoms in May, always to be the gala month of this tiny theatre.

It was just a week before the breaking-up that Wendy discovered the reason why Cassandra had not tried to win the classical scholarship.

Isobel had done such steady and excellent work that there could be no doubt in any one's mind that she would gain the honour; but when Wendy called her to the sanctum to tell her this she burst out with, "It's too splendid for words, but of course I could *never* have passed Laurette without Cassandra."

"Cassandra!"

"Yes; you see, Miss Wendell, things are rather unlucky at home just now. The boys cost such an awful lot that Dad said I must leave school this term and study at home as well as I could, which would have been hateful, and quite impossible if I take up teaching, as I mean to if I can. I told Cassandra and she said she wasn't trying for the scholarship and would coach me. She's been wonderful, and I'm so frightfully glad to think I can stay at Idle Pines another whole year."

"I'm glad, too, dear. It was nice of Cassandra to help you and you've worked *splendidly*. Now will you run and tell Cassandra I want her."

Cassandra came, looking rather doleful, for there were moments when her disappointment about the scholarship plunged her into one of her gloomy moods.

"Cassandra, dear, well played!"

Cassandra flushed. Those were the words her father always used when he was particularly pleased with one of them.

"But what have I done, Wendy? You haven't been pleased with my Latin for weeks and weeks."

"No, I have not; and I won't have any more of it, remember that next term, my child; but I've just been talking to Isobel."

Cassandra went scarlet and mumbled, "What an idiot Isobel is."

"No, she's not; she's a nice, clever girl and I'm so glad you've made a friend of her, Cassandra. I know your father would rather you gained a friend than a scholarship—he had such a genius for friendship himself and it worried him when you stood so much aloof from other girls. In fact, I think turning Idle Pines into a school has been good for all four of you; a little responsibility has made Penelope wake up so successfully she takes more burdens off my shoulders every day. Cassandra has made a life-long friendship and doesn't prophesy family disasters so frequently! Pandora is less harum-scarum and not so fond of poking her fingers into other people's pies, and Rory is not such a little fury and is learning to control herself."

"Wendy, is it a secret about the silver medal? Laurette *ought* to have it, I know."

"And so she will; but remember, Cassandra, that next year I expect it to remain in the family, so don't give me any more weak verses, please."

"And Penelope has got the *cordon bleu*!"

"She deserves it. Now give me a kiss and let me finish my work. I feel quite distracted with so much to do before the fifth."

Cassandra went away as happy as a queen, for praise from Wendy was rare and precious, and somehow she felt she had won something better than a scholarship.

A country fête was to be held in the grounds of Idle Pines on the fifth of May, and as usual Wendy left the drawing up of the programme of attractions entirely to the girls.

Penelope and Eve, with a few attendant juniors, decided to be dairymaids in pink print frocks and sell butter, eggs, cheese, and cream in a green bower on the north lawn.

Mary Leslie and her industrious seven erected a fairy-well in the rose garden, into which they put all the pretty things they had been making for months past, knowing it would delight the country youths to fish for a fairing for some favoured village maiden.

Laurette ingeniously built a stall shaped like a beehive under the apple trees in the orchard, where she intended to sell jars of heather honey, and Isobel and the fourth patrol made dozens of tiny packets of dried herbs, lavender bags, and pots of *pot-pourri*. Their stall was to be in the herb garden near the dove-cote and the sellers were to be attired in Puritan dresses.

"Well, I'm perfectly certain I can't think of a thing to do," said Cassandra rather crossly to her followers.

"Couldn't we have a wax-work show of Greek statues?" said Jill helpfully; but the suggestion was coldly received by Cassandra, who had not forgotten her last attempt to amuse people with Greek statuary.

Then, once more, Pandora had an idea. She suggested that the Sanctuary should be turned into a tiny inn for one afternoon, with Cassandra as hostess and Jill, Julie, Rory, and herself as serving maids.

They painted a wooden sign with a picture of the woodland house upon it and the words "To Greenwood Inn" underneath. This was hung upon a pine-tree near the bowling green, and any one who wandered down a gorse-scented forest path would come upon a charming country inn.

"We'll make the teas frightfully expensive," said Jill. "They ought to pay lots for taking sanctuary from the crowd and village kids eating sticky buns," and, as everybody agreed with her, they gleefully prepared for making a fortune.

Wendy and Miss Dillon had a pottery stall, Madame Clément and Miss Bruce were to sell baskets and flowers, and long tea tables were to be spread under the cedar-tree, presided over by Mary Ellen and the maids, for those who could not afford the luxuries of Greenwood Inn.

Dorothy had charge of the sports and games in the paddock, and Aunt Sally announced her intention of pitching her tent in the kitchen garden and selling potatoes and good honest bunches of carrots, turnips, and onions.

"The stalls and tea will all be nice, I think," said

Larette, "but I'm afraid there are not enough amuse-ments."

"Let's have another play," cried Jill and Pandora together.

"Not with *you* in it, after the way you behaved last time," said Eve, ready to administer a snub, and Laurette added: "Besides, the Players and Singers are doing a play, and we don't want to bore people by too much of that sort of thing; we must all try to think of something else."

Jill's "set," as Pauline still called it, put their heads together and thought earnestly. Then they approached Cassandra, and, with flattering allusions to her dramatic talent, asked her to write them a Red Indian pageant.

"A Red Indian pageant! Don't be absurd."

"It isn't absurd. Do listen, Cassandra. It really is a lovely idea," coaxed Pandora. "From the seats on the bowling green you can see right into the pine wood, and it would be so exciting to give something really thrilling with the ponies, you know, after the play."

"I suppose you mean something like that film you were so mad about, that you saw in the Forest," said Cassandra. "Don't be silly; Wendy would hate it. All the same, it isn't a bad idea to have a sort of spectacle in the pine wood. I'll talk to Laurette about it."

The next day Cassandra announced that if they would promise to be sensible and do nothing silly she would help them to arrange two scenes on the death of William Rufus in the New Forest. They would act these scenes in the pine wood, while she stood on the stage of the theatre and recited the old ballad about this historical incident.

"*Rufus!*" said the would-be film star dolefully, and Jill added: "I say, Cassandra, couldn't you pump out something about a more exciting sort of Redskin than Rufus?"

"No, I couldn't," answered Cassandra indignantly. "I chose him because you can have the hunting scene and use the ponies, and you ought to be very grateful, especially as I've asked Wendy if you can do it, and she says you may. We have got dresses, too, for the king and the courtiers, and all we want for the Saxon churls are a few sacks for tunics, sandals, and some girls with bobbed hair."

Striving to appear grateful, the girls accepted Cassandra's kind offer to help, although, to tell the truth, they had hoped to thrill their audience with more exciting scenes.

The hero of the film had lassoed two Indians with such amazing skill that Jill and Pandora decided they would begin to practise this fascinating art, so that if they were ever lucky enough to be attacked by brigands they could despatch them in the true, heroic way. This they did so successfully that before long they could lasso Julie and Rory while running at full speed, and now they naturally burned to show off such an accomplishment.

Rory suggested that it would bring more excitement into Cassandra's historical scene if Rufus were to be lassoed, instead of slain with the traditional arrow, but even Jill owned that this idea was a trifle *too* daring.

"The first scene is the king hunting on the morning of Lammas Day," said Cassandra, at the first rehearsal. "Julie, you'll have to be the monk who stops him on his way and gives him warning that evil will befall him if he hunts on a holy day."

"But that's a dull part," objected Julie.

"It won't be dull if *I'm* Rufus," promised Pandora in an undertone. "Don't say anything to Cassandra, but, if you like, I'll try to trample you down. Or you can be dragged along holding on to Redskin's mane; he won't mind—the angel!"

Jill was to be Sir Walter Tyrell, and Rory a page in

attendance on the king. She had decided to make the part exciting by turning Jackyboy into a fiery steed, and she was also to play the part of William Purkiss in the second scene and, with the help of a few more Saxon churls, bear away the royal corpse to Winchester.

The Fifth dawned hot and radiant.

The money made at the fête was to benefit the Country Holiday Fund for poor children and the "Dispensaries for Sick Animals of the Poor," a noble charity in which Miss Caird, Wendy, and the girls were deeply interested.

The lucky "angels" of Idle Pines were expected to do their share for their suffering brethren, and the dogs and cats all had tin boxes round their necks for donations, and the ponies, gaily beribboned and saddled, stood tethered in a row in the paddock, ready to be hired out by girl and boy visitors for a ten minutes' ride.

Bluebell did her part too, and sat on a flowery throne dressed as a May Queen, crowned with bluebells and attended by eight pretty village maidens, who offered bunches of her name flower and a kiss from their rosy, chuckling queen, for the small sum of one penny.

"I do hope crowds come," said Gladys; "anyhow, Poppa is sure to turn up."

"Joe says lots of people will go to the Wild Beast Show that's pitched in Berry's field," said Pandora dolefully.

"A Wild Beast Show—how gorgeous!" cried Julie; "I wish *we* could go."

"Hateful people shutting up those darling lions and tigers in cages and stuffy tents to be stared at," said Rory, almost weeping.

"I'd rather like to see Buddha, the ape," said Jill. "Joe says he rides a bicycle and washes up the teacups in the rummiest way."

They were all carrying chairs and benches to the bowling green after a hurried luncheon, and Joe came round the corner at that moment with a wheel-barrow full of flowers for the stage.

"Heared the news, missy?" he inquired.

"No; do tell us, Joe."

"That there ape from the Show yonder, he be escaped."

"Escaped! Not really! how awful!" cried the girls.

"Yes, he be; a girt, wild sassy brute a-chockvul of mischief, and the folk down in the village in a fine to-do. This marning he came down from the big elum tree and jumped clean on to Annie Barrett's back when she wor fetching the milk avore breakfast. The little wench has taken fits with the fright and all, they say; he clawed her awful, but keepers can't catch 'un."

This was exciting news, but with so much to do the girls had no time to discuss it any further with the loquacious Joe.

The Forest Singers and Players opened the Fête with an exciting smuggling play in which Joe turned out to be a better actor than gardener, but he delivered his lines so slowly that Aunt Sally became annoyed and cried out, "Don't forget there's the pigs to feed at half-past four, my lad, so get on with your smuggling, for goodness' sake!"

The Rufus episode was the next item on the programme, and the actors behind the pine-trees awaited their turn with feverish impatience.

Pandora, as Rufus, was richly clad in crimson and purple and was mounted on Redskin, gaily caparisoned. Jill was a handsome Sir Walter in dark green, and Rory made a gay little royal page in scarlet. Diana and Mavis were courtiers, and Julie, clad in her monkish habit, sat under a tree surrounded by a group of "ordinaries" attired as Saxon churls.

"There are *crowds* of people," cried Rory, peeping through the trees.

"Millions," said Jill. "I say, do look at that precious child!"

The "precious child," the adored school baby, had left her flowery throne and was sitting in front of the audience on a large rug spread on the grass, surrounded by her maids of honour.

"*Treasure!*" cried Pandora. "Look here, Jill, Cassandra says we mustn't stop to unsaddle the ponies when it's over, but simply fly and change, because of the Greenwood Inn teas. We had better keep these lassoes and use them for tethering them until Joe comes. They won't show."

The coils of rope used for their Indian games were tied to their saddles, and they tucked them out of sight under the purple and crimson trappings.

Loud clapping proclaimed the play was over, and Cassandra rushed up and ordered the actors in the first scene to be in readiness. Then she flew off to take her place upon the stage.

To make the scene more impressive, it was arranged that the cavalcade should appear as far back as possible in the distance of the wood. Keeping well out of sight, Pandora led the way, followed by her courtiers, Rory in the rear.

A stifled scream from the royal page made the ponies rear, and the king and his courtiers wheeled round in consternation to see an extraordinary sight. Rory was seated bolt upright on Jackyboy, who was plunging wildly and sitting behind her, grinning hideously, was a large, hairy ape.

He was more like an old man of the woods than a monkey, for his wrinkled black face was fringed with whiskers, his arms were long and hairy, and the chattering noise he made sounded like the unintelligible mumblings of an old man.

Rory, as white as death, kept her seat on the terrified,

rearing pony, even when the ape plucked the scarlet cap from her head, but before any one could come to the rescue he jumped to the ground and climbed up a pine-tree, chattering horribly.

"Oh, Pan," said Rory faintly, "the wood is going round and round and I feel sick——"

"No, you don't," said Pandora firmly. "In a minute the horn will sound and we *must* go on."

"Look here," said Jill, "Pandora, oughtn't we to get somebody to catch that awful brute?"

"No," answered Pandora emphatically; "we *must* go on now: it's safe up that tree until the scene's over."

A huntsman's horn rang out suddenly—the signal for the procession to appear in sight, and with an encouraging word of praise to poor Rory, Rufus and his courtiers rode out into the glade.

Before they had advanced fifty yards, Jill, riding close to the king, whispered, "Oh, Pan, look—the ape! It's coming along with us!"

To Pandora's dismay, she saw the hideous ape ambling along in the undergrowth close to them.

"Don't tell the others; keep on," she whispered, and, to their joy, the creature suddenly disappeared amongst the thick trees behind the theatre.

On they came, but before Redskin's hoofs had touched the turf of the bowling green, Pandora saw a sight which almost transfixed her with horror. The ape had reappeared at the other side of the theatre and was actually squatting on the turf, its long, hairy arms clasped round its knees, its hideous face grimacing horribly, *not thirty yards away from the precious school baby!*

Jill saw it at the same moment and her face went white with terror, for through the minds of both girls flashed Joe's words: "The little wench has taken fits with the fright and all; he clawed her awful!"

The strange thing was that not a single person in the

audience saw the creature, for every eye was fixed on the gay company advancing through the wood.

"Oh, Pan," moaned Jill, "what shall we do?"

"Hush! We must think of something." Then, with sudden inspiration, Pandora cried, "Jill, we've got the lassoes! Do you think——?"

In a flash Jill caught her meaning and nodded.

"Yes, we can. I'll tell the others to stand still," and, turning swiftly, she gave the order to the astonished courtiers.

Cassandra, standing on the stage, dramatically reciting the tale of that Lammas Day of long ago, was amazed to see the procession suddenly stop, instead of riding past the stage slowly to reappear at the other side of the wood in the chase of the white hart.

She saw Rufus advance alone, fumbling at his purple trappings; then through the air flashed a coil of rope, so swiftly and gracefully thrown that it looked like a wreath of smoke uncurling as it sped on its way.

Then a slender figure in dark green flew forward on a chestnut horse, and another coil of rope flashed through the air, and a wild scream of rage and terror made every one rise in their seats to watch the extraordinary sight of two girls sitting firmly upon plunging steeds, each holding a rope which firmly pinioned the body and arms of a struggling, hairy ape!

There were screams from the villagers too.

"The ape! The ape! That's 'un that's give fits to Barrett's little wench. To think of that now, and only two young lassies they be! Who'll fetch keepers, Missus?"

Wendy, very pale, hastened to join those of the audience who had flown to the rescue.

"Colonel Wrench, what must I do?" she asked a friend and neighbour.

"*Do?* Send your man off to fetch the brute's owner,

I suppose, and lock it in the stable until they come. Look here, Miss Wendell—if you won't think it rude of me to say so—I was dragged here by my wife, 'pon my honour I was, and expected to hear recitations from a row of schoolgirls, but I wouldn't have missed this for pounds. Lassoing, by Jove! A nice accomplishment for young ladies! Do tell me if you put it in your prospectus?"

But Wendy was too much worried to smile at old Colonel Wrench's jokes. In a few minutes she had despatched Joe to fetch the showman, while the Colonel, with more volunteers from the audience than he needed, conducted the ape, now cringing and crying like a baby, to the safe shelter of the coach house.

Wendy then calmed the excited audience with a few quiet words. Begging them to take their seats again she assured them that the dangerous creature was now captured, and that the historical pageant, which it appearance had unfortunately interrupted, was now ready to begin again.

Neither of the heroines had found it so enjoyable as she had anticipated to play the part of chief actor in an exciting scene. In fact, they both looked pale and shaky when Wendy whispered, "Carry on, like good girls."

But in a few minutes the huntsman's horn again heralded the approach of the gay cavalcade, and as Rufus, Sir Walter, and poor capless Rory rode by jauntily, the enthusiastic cheers that greeted them encouraged them to play their parts so well that even the critical Cassandra was proud of them.

Rufus, pierced by Sir Walter's arrow, fell from his horse dramatically and lay with outstretched hands still and quiet under the pine-trees, until a group of Saxon peasants came up the glade with a rough wooden-wheeled cart.

Rory, as Purkiss, the charcoal burner, looked almost tragic as she knelt by the fallen king, but it was not for the royal victim she wept—her tears were for an ugly ape, bound and imprisoned in the cold coach house, for even vicious monkeys in distress were "angels" to the tender-hearted Rory.

The bearing of the dead king's body through the wood on its way to Winchester brought the pageant to a dramatic finish, and the actors in it were loudly applauded.

Then Wendy appeared on the stage and made a charming speech to the audience, explaining the aims of the Singers and Players, and how the Guild had been founded through an idea of one of her pupils. She hoped that every one would work for its advancement; and she suggested that a manager should be elected, and that any play sent in should be read carefully and produced if worthy of the honour, however young the author might be!

She then presented Laurette with the silver medal, Penelope with the *cordon bleu*, and announced that Isobel was the winner of the Richard Charles Barron Scholarship.

Before the audience dispersed Wendy was able to announce that Buddha, the ape, had been claimed by his owner, and that no village maids need tremble on their homeward way.

Rory was enraptured with the proprietor of the Wild Beast Show, who turned out to be a most humane person and petted the wicked Buddha in the most indulgent way.

"He's only a young 'un, ma'am," he explained to Wendy, "and full of beans, as the saying is. I'm sure I'm very much obliged to your young ladies for catching him without damaging him—he's a valuable animal, ma'am; and if you'll allow Buddha to give a trifle to this 'ere charity, I'm sure I'll be pround to offer it."

He presented the delightful Jill and Pandora with five guineas for the Fund, and really, for once, Wendy did not know whether to scold or praise them!

There was then a rush for the fragrant cups of tea Mary Ellen was dispensing under the cedar-tree, and to the delights of Greenwood Inn.

Cassandra rushed about with her four rosy maids, serving tea, home made bread and butter, thick cream and strawberry jam, on small tables set under the pine-trees outside the inn. Jessie Mills presided over a row of boiling kettles in the kitchen, and Satan, with a green bow tied under his black chin, sat on the doorstep, prepared to be angelic to any guest willing to share the contents of the cream-jug with him.

When tea and sports were over there were country dances and old English games for every one on the big lawn, while the village band played under the cedar-tree and old Miss Caird sat and chuckled with delight.

The last reveller left the gates of Idle Pines long after "the-youngest-girl-in-the-school" had been taken to bed with her bluebell crown drooping over her curly head, decidedly cross, but with a lapful of sixpences and pennies for poor girls who could never be queens.

To the delight of the workers, all the stalls were empty and all the money-boxes full; and there was a triumphant supper party under the big cedar-tree at the end of the day, which all the "angels" shared, for they had done their parts, too, and collected lots and lots by just looking adorable, as Rory pointed out when she emptied the sugar-bowl for the ponies, and piled a row of saucers and plates on the lawn with all the tit-bits she could collect.

After supper, Wendy led the way to the big school-room, where they had all first gathered together on that May evening a year ago, with its open windows looking over the golden gorse and the misty blue of the sea.

But there was a difference. Girls and mistresses drew together as comrades who had worked and played together with the good fellowship Wendy had so much desired in Idle Pines. And nobody could have wished for a sturdier family; for the bright eyes and rosy cheeks on all sides proved that a Spartan training brings its own reward.

Nobody whispered that Wendy looked "dowdy," and even Pauline acknowledged she *was* a Personage, as Pandora had said.

Gladys Shaw, brown and slender, was too fond of Aunt Sally to see anything "comic" in her absurd little hat and flannel shirt, and the whole school felt proud of Miss Dillon.

Wendy called the roll, and then, smiling rather whimsically, she said: "Well, children, the year of probation is over, and I find I cannot spare one of you; but if any of you want to leave Idle Pines you have now the right to go. Suppose we say hands up for all who wish to stay."

Every hand went up, with such cheers for Wendy and Idle Pines that for a moment she could not speak; then Penelope rose and, in her pretty, shy way, said:

"Wendy, of *course* we all want to stay, and we remember all you said a year ago and see you were right in everything. There is only one request you made that we really can't agree to"—she looked round at all the girls mischievously—"we really and truly *must* call you ' a perfect darling.' "

And the whole school stood up and roared with applause.

THE END